The Sign of the Beaver

OTHER YEARLING BOOKS YOU WILL ENJOY:

YEARLING BOOKS/YOUNG YEARLINGS/YEARLING CLASSICS are designed especially to entertain and enlighten young people. Patricia Reilly Giff, consultant to this series, received her bachelor's degree from Marymount College and a master's degree in history from St. John's University. She holds a Professional Diploma in Reading and a Doctorate of Humane Letters from Hofstra University. She was a teacher and reading consultant for many years, and is the author of numerous books for young readers.

For a complete listing of all Yearling titles, write to
Dell Readers Service,
P.O. Box 1045,
South Holland, IL 60473.

The Sign of the Beaver

Elizabeth George Speare

A LITTLE YEARLING BOOK

Published by
Dell Publishing
a division of
Bantam Doubleday Dell Publishing Group, Inc.
1540 Broadway
New York, New York 10036

To William and Michael

The trademark Yearling® is registered in the U.S. Patent and Trademark Office.

The trademark Dell® is registered in the U.S. Patent and Trademark Office.

ISBN: 0-440-77903-0

Reprinted by arrangement with Houghton Mifflin Company

Printed in the United States of America

June 1993

30 29 28 27 26 25

RAD

The Sign of the Beaver

CHAPTER 1

MATT STOOD AT THE EDGE OF THE CLEARING FOR some time after his father had gone out of sight among the trees. There was just a chance that his father might turn back, that perhaps he had forgotten something or had some last word of advice. This was one time Matt reckoned he wouldn't mind the advice, no matter how many times he had heard it before. But finally he had to admit that this was not going to happen. His father had really gone. He was alone, with miles of wilderness stretching on every side.

He turned and looked back at the log house. It was a fair house, he thought; his mother would have no cause to be ashamed of it. He had helped to build every inch of it. He had helped to cut down the spruce trees and haul the logs and square and notch them. He had stood at one end of every log and raised it, one on top of the other, fitting the notched ends together as snugly as though they had grown that way. He had climbed the roof to fasten down the cedar splints with long poles, and dragged up pine boughs to cover them. Behind the cabin were the mounds of corn he had helped to plant, the green blades already shooting up, and the pumpkin vines just showing between the stumps of trees.

If only it were not so quiet. He had been alone before. His father had often gone into the forest to hunt, for hours on end. Even when he was there, he was not much of a talker. Sometimes they had worked side by side through a whole morning without his speaking a single word. But this silence was different. It coiled around Matt and reached into his stomach to settle there in a hard knot.

He knew it was high time his father was starting back. This was part of the plan that the family had worked out together in the long winter of 1768, sitting by lamplight around the pine table back in Massachusetts. His father had spread out the surveyor's map and traced the boundaries of the land he had purchased in Maine territory. They would be the first settlers in a new township. In the spring, when the ice melted, Matt and his father would travel north. They would take passage on a ship to the settlement at the mouth of the Penobscot River. There they would find some man with a boat to take them up the river and then on up a smaller river that branched off from it, many days' distance from the settlement. Finally they would strike out on foot into the forest and claim their own plot of land. They would clear a patch of ground, build a cabin, and plant some corn. In the summer his father would go back to Massachusetts to fetch his mother and sister and the new baby, who would be born while they were gone. Matt would stay behind and guard the cabin and the corn patch.

It hadn't been quite so easy as it had sounded back in their house in Quincy. Matt had had to get used to going to sleep at night with every muscle in his body aching. But the log house was finished. It had only one room. Before winter they would add a loft for him and his sister to sleep in. Inside there were shelves along one wall and a sturdy puncheon table with two stools. One of these days, his father promised, he would cut out a window and fasten oiled paper to let in the light. Someday the paper would be replaced with real glass. Against the wall was a chimney of smaller logs, daubed and lined with clay from the creek. This too was a temporary structure. Over and over his father had warned Matt that it wasn't as safe as a stone chimney and that he had to watch out for flying sparks. He needn't fear. After all the work of building this house, Matt wasn't going to let it burn down about his ears.

"Six weeks," his father had said that morning. "Maybe seven. Hard to reckon exactly. With your ma and sister we'll have slow going, specially with the new little one.

"You may lose track of the weeks," he had added. "Easy thing to do when you're alone. Might be well to make notches on a stick, seven notches to a stick. When you get to the seventh stick you can start looking for us."

A silly thing to do, Matt thought, as though he couldn't count the weeks for himself. But he wouldn't argue about it, not on the last morning.

Then his father reached up to a chink in the log wall and took down the battered tin box that held his watch and his compass and a few silver coins. He took out the big silver watch.

"Every time you cut a notch," he said, "remember to wind this up at the same time."

3

Matt took the watch in his hand as gently as if it were a bird's egg. "You aim to leave it, Pa?" he asked.

"It belonged to your grandpa. Would've belonged to you anyhow sooner or later. Might as well be now."

"You mean — it's mine?"

"Aye, it's yourn. Be kind of company, hearing it tick."

The lump in Matt's throat felt as big as the watch. This was the finest thing his father had ever possessed.

"I'll take care of it," he managed finally.

"Aye. I knowed you would. Mind you don't wind it up too tight."

Then, just before he left, his father had given him a second gift. Thinking of it, Matt walked back into the cabin and looked up at his father's rifle, hanging on two pegs over the door.

"I'll take your old blunderbuss with me," his father had said. "This one aims truer. But mind you, don't go banging away at everything that moves. Wait till you're dead sure. There's plenty of powder if you don't waste it."

It was the first sign he had given that he felt uneasy about leaving Matt here alone. Matt wished now that he could have said something to reassure his father, instead of standing there tongue-tied. But if he had the chance again, he knew he wouldn't do any better. They just weren't a family to put things into words.

He reached up and took down the rifle. It was lighter than his old matchlock, the one his father had carried away with him in exchange. This was a fine piece, the walnut stock as smooth and shining as his mother's silk

4

droop. It was a mile long, but it had a good balance. With this gun he wouldn't need to waste powder. So it wouldn't hurt to take one shot right now, just to try the feel of it.

He knew his father always kept that rifle as clean as a new-polished spoon. But because he enjoyed handling it, Matt poked about in the touchhole with the metal pick. From the powder horn he shook a little of the black powder into the pan. Then he took one lead bullet out of the pouch, wrapped it in a patch of cloth, and rammed it into the barrel. As he worked, he whistled loudly into the stillness. It made the knot in his stomach loosen a little.

As he stepped into the woods, a bluejay screeched a warning. So it was some time before he spotted anything to shoot at. Presently he saw a red squirrel hunched on a branch, with its tail curled up behind its ears. He lifted the rifle and sighted along the barrel, minding his father's advice and waiting till he was dead sure.

The clean feel of the shot delighted him. It didn't set him back on his heels like his old matchlock. Still, he hadn't quite got the knack of it. He caught the flick of a tail as the squirrel scampered to an upper branch.

I could do better with my own gun, he thought. This rifle of his father's was going to take some getting used to.

Ruefully he trudged back to the cabin. For his noon meal he sat munching a bit of the johnnycake his father had baked that morning. Already he was beginning to realize that time was going to move slowly. A whole afternoon to go before he could cut that first notch.

Seven sticks. That would be August. He would have a birthday before August. He supposed his father had forgotten that, with so many things on his mind. By the time his family got here, he would be thirteen years old.

⊸⅋CHAPTER 2⅋⊸

By the next morning the tight place in his stomach was gone. By the morning after that Matt decided that it was mighty pleasant living alone. He enjoyed waking to a day stretched before him to fill as he pleased. He could set himself the necessary chores without having to listen to any advice about how they should be done. How could he have thought that the time would move slowly? As the days passed and he cut one notch after another on his stick, Matt discovered that there was never time enough for all that must be done between sunrise and sunset.

Although the cabin was finished, his father had left him the endless task of chinking the spaces between the logs with clay from the creek bank. At the edge of the clearing there were trees to fell to let in more sun on the growing corn, and underbrush that kept creeping closer over the cleared ground. All this provided plenty of wood to be chopped and stacked in the woodpile against the cabin wall.

To cook a meal for himself once or twice a day, he had to keep a fire going. Twice in the first few days he had waked and found the ashes cold. Back home in Quincy, if his mother's fire burned out she had sent

7

him or Sarah with her shovel to borrow a live coal from a neighbor. There was no neighbor here. He had to gather twigs and make a wad of shredded cedar bark, then strike his flint and blow on the tiny spark until it burst into flame. A man could get mighty hungry before he had coaxed that spark into a cooking fire.

The corn patch needed constant tending. In these hot, bright days, every drop of water that those green shoots demanded had to be lugged from the creek, a kettleful at a time, and there was no way to water the corn without encouraging the weeds as well. As fast as he pulled them, new ones sprang up. The crows drove him distracted, forever flapping about. A dozen times a day he would dash at them fiercely, shouting and waving his arms. They would just fly lazily off and wait on a nearby treetop till his back was turned. He dared not waste his precious powder on them. At night wild creatures nibbled the tops of the green shoots. Once he sat up all night with his rifle across his knees, batting at the mosquitoes. When morning came he stumbled into the cabin and slept away half the day. That was the second time he let the fire go out.

He seemed to be hungrier than ever before in his life. The barrel of flour was going down almost as fast as when two were dipping into it. He depended on his gun to keep his stomach filled. He was still proud of that gun, but no longer in awe of it. Carrying it over his shoulder, he set out confidently into the forest, venturing farther each day, certain of bringing home a duck or a rabbit for his dinner. For a change of diet

8

he could take his fish pole and follow the twisting course of the creek or walk the trail his father had blazed to a pond some distance away. In no time he could catch all the fish he could eat. Twice he had glimpsed a deer moving through the trees just out of range of his rifle. One of these days, he promised himself, he would bring one down.

It was a good life, with only a few small annoyances buzzing like mosquitoes inside his head. One of these was the thought of Indians. Not that he feared them. His father had been assured by the proprietors that his new settlement would be safe. Since the last treaty with the tribes, there had not been an attack reported anywhere in this part of Maine. Still, one could not entirely forget all those horrid tales. And he just didn't like the feeling he had sometimes that someone was watching him. He couldn't prove it. He could never see anything more than a quick shadow that might be a moving branch. But he couldn't shake off the feeling that someone was there.

One of those pieces of advice his father had been so fond of giving him had been about Indians. "They won't bother you," he said. "Most of 'em have left for Canada. The ones who stayed don't want to make any trouble. But Indians take great stock in politeness. Should you meet one, speak to him just the same as to the minister back home."

Matt had seen his father follow his own advice. Once, when they had tramped a long way from the cabin, they had seen in the distance a solitary dark-skinned figure. The two men had nodded to each other gravely, and lifted a hand in salute, exactly as if they had been two deacons passing in the town square. But how could you be respectful to a shadow that would not show itself? It made Matt uneasy.

He had grown used to the stillness. In fact he knew now that the forest is rarely quiet. As he tramped through it he was accompanied by the chirruping of birds, the chatter of squirrels, and the whine and twang of thousands of bothersome insects. In the night he could recognize now the strange sounds that used to startle him. The grunt of a porcupine rummaging in the garden. The boom of the great horned owl. The scream of some small creature pounced upon in the forest. Or the long, quavering cry of the loon from the distant pond. The first time he had heard that loon call he had thought it was a wolf. Now he liked to hear it. Mournful as it was, it was the cry of another living creature. Matt would worm his shoulder into a comfortable spot in the hemlock boughs that made his mattress, pull the blanket over his head to shut out the mosquitoes, and fall asleep well satisfied with his world.

He would have liked, however, to have someone to talk to occasionally. He hadn't reckoned on missing that. For much of the day he was content to be alone, tramping through the woods or sitting on the bank of the creek dangling his fishline. He was like his father in that. But there were times when he had a thought he'd like to share with someone. With anybody. Even his sister, Sarah, though he'd never paid much mind to her at home.

So he was not so quick-witted as he should have been when unexpectedly someone arrived.

~&CHAPTER 3&~

HE WAS SITTING ON THE FLAT STONE THAT SERVED
as a doorstep, waiting for his supper to cook. The late
sun slanted in long yellow bars across the clearing. The
forest beyond was already in shadow. Matt was feeling
well pleased with his day. That morning he had shot
a rabbit. He had skinned it carefully, stretching the fur
against the cabin wall to dry. Chunks of the meat were
boiling now in the kettle over the fire, and the good
smell came through the door and made his mouth water.

In the dimness of the trees, a darker shadow moved.
This time it didn't disappear but came steadily nearer.
He could hear the crackle of twigs under heavy boots.
Matt leaped to his feet.

"Pa!"

No answer. It wasn't his father, of course. It couldn't
be. An Indian? Matt felt a curl of alarm against his
backbone. He stood waiting, his muscles tensed.

The man who came tramping out from the trees was
not an Indian. He was heavyset, the fat bulging under
a ragged blue army coat. His face was almost invisible
behind a tangle of reddish whiskers. Halfway across
the clearing he stopped.

"Howdy!" he called cheerfully.

"Hello," Matt answered uncertainly. Was this some-one who ought to be greeted like a deacon?

The stranger came closer, so that Matt could see the small blue eyes that glittered in the weather-hardened face. The man stood, deliberately taking his time, look-ing over the cabin and the cornfield.

"Nice place you got here."

Matt said nothing.

The man peered curiously over Matt's shoulder through the open door. He could easily see that the cabin was empty.

"You all alone here?"

Matt hesitated. "My father is away just now."

"Be back soon, will he?"

Matt was puzzled by his own unwillingness to answer. He ought to be glad to see anyone after all these days alone, but somehow he wasn't. He didn't quite know why he found himself lying.

"Anytime now," he said. "He went back to the river to get supplies. He might be back tonight. When I saw you coming I thought it was him."

"Guess I surprised you. Reckon you don't get much company way off here."

"No, we don't," Matt answered.

"Then your pappy wouldn't want you to turn away a visitor, would he?" the man asked. "Thought mebbe you'd ask me to stay for supper. I got a whiff of it half a mile off."

Matt remembered his manners. The man's easy grin was beginning to wipe away some of his doubts. "Of course," he said. "Come in — sir."

The man snorted. "Ben's the name," he said. "You may of heard of me in the river town."

"We didn't stay in the town very long," Matt answered. He hurried now to light a candle. The stranger stood inside the door, taking in every inch of the small room.

"Your pappy knows how to build a good, tight house," he said. "You reckon on staying here for good?"

"It's our land," Matt told him. In the candlelight the room looked snug and homey, something to be proud of showing off to a stranger. "My mother and sister will be coming soon."

"More folks comin' all the time," the man said. "Time was you could tramp for a month and never see a chimney. Now the towns is spreading out from the river every which way."

His eye fell on the rifle hanging over the door. He let out a slow, admiring whistle and walked over to run his hand along the stock. "Mighty fine piece," he said. "Worth a passel of beaver."

"My father wouldn't sell it," Matt said shortly. He was busying himself now to make this stranger welcome. He scooped out a good measure of flour, stirred in some water, patted the dough out on a clean ash board, and propped it up in front of the fire to bake. He laid out the two bowls on the table and the two pewter spoons. He poured molasses into the one pewter dish. Then he ladled the hot stew into the bowls.

The way that stew disappeared, the stranger couldn't have eaten a meal for a good while. Matt took a very small share for himself. He pulled back his hand and watched the man snatch the last bit of corn cake, sopping up the last of the molasses with it. Finally Ben pushed back his stool and drew the back of his hand across his beard.

"That was mighty tasty, son. Mighty tasty. You wouldn't have a mite of tobacco now, would you?"

"I'm sorry," Matt said. "My father doesn't have any."

"Pity. Can't be helped, I suppose."

In the easy silence that followed, Matt decided to ask a question of his own. "Are you traveling to the river?"

Ben snorted again. "Not likely. I'm keeping as fur off from that river's I can, till things quiet down."

Matt waited.

"Tell the truth, I got away from that town just in time. Warn't nothin' they could prove, but they sure had it in for me. So I says, Ben, I says, you been plannin' on gettin' yourself some beaver pelts. Looks like now's the time to get moving. I aim to settle in with the redskins a bit, maybe move on north."

"You mean you're going to live with the Indians?"

"Could do worse. I can bed down 'bout anywheres."

It certainly looked as though, invited or not, Ben was planning on bedding down right here in the cabin. He had eased himself off the stool and sprawled out on the floor, his shoulders propped against the wall. He pulled a dirty corncob pipe from his pocket and stared down at it ruefully.

"Pity," he said again. "Meal like that needs 'baccy to settle it right." He put the pipe away and shifted his heavy bulk against the wall.

"When I was not much more'n your age," he drawled,

well-fed and ready to talk, "I'd spend the whole winter with the redskins. Hunt with 'em, trap. Easy to pick up their lingo. Still remember a deal of it. But this country ain't the same anymore. You got to go west, Ohio mebbe, to get any decent trapping."

"The Indians still hunt here, don't they?" Matt asked.

"The Indians has mostly cleared out of these parts," Ben told him. "What wasn't killed off in the war got took with the sickness. A deal of 'em moved on to Canada. What's left makes a mighty poor living, game gettin' so scarce."

"Where do they live?"

"Round about." Ben waved vaguely toward the forest. "They make small camps for a while and then move on. The Penobscots stick like burrs, won't give up. They still hunt and trap. No way to stop 'em. Never got it through their heads they don't still own this land. You never seen none of 'em?"

"My father did once. Do they speak English?"

"Enough to get what they want. They pick it up from the traders. What pelts they can scrape together they take into the towns. They can strike a sharp deal. You got to know how to handle 'em.

"Reason you ain't seen 'em," he went on, "they got enough sense to clear out of these parts when the bugs is bad. They move off, the whole lot, down to the coast to get their year's mess of clams. Should be movin' back 'bout now. They'll stay the summer and then go off for the big hunt come fall.

"Them hunts," he remembered. "Ain't nothin' like 'em nowadays. Bows and arrows was all they had. Still use 'em some, if they can't lay hands on a gun. I got so's I was demmed near as good as any of 'em. Don't suppose I could hit a barn door now."

Ben's voice drawled on and on, thickened with food and drowsiness. He told of the big moose hunts of his days with the Indians. He had fought in the recent war against the French and he despised them for stirring up the Indians against the Maine settlements. He seemed to have singlehandedly shot down half the French army. Especially he hated the Jesuit priests who had egged the redskins on, and he had once been part of an expedition that broke into a chapel and smashed the popish idols. Once he had been taken captive by the fierce Iroquois, who were set on putting him to torture, but he had been too smart for them and escaped in the night. Listening, Matt couldn't make the man out. To hear him talk, he had been as big a hero as Jack the Giant Killer, but he didn't look the part. He had certainly fallen on hard times of late. No doubt about it, however, he could tell a good story.

The man's voice was trailing off, and he slumped lower and lower. Presently he was sprawled flat on the floor and snoring. It was clear enough that he could bed down anywhere. At least he hadn't taken over Matt's bed.

Matt moved about quietly, though he doubted anything could disturb his guest. He cleaned off the bowls with his twig brush. Then he banked the fire with ashes. Finally he settled down on his hemlock mattress.

But he couldn't sleep. He lay staring up at the log roof, even after the last flickers of firelight had died away and the cabin was in darkness. He couldn't quiet his uneasy thoughts. Bragging about his adventures by the fire, Ben had seemed harmless, just a fat, tired old man grateful for a good meal. To be honest, Matt had enjoyed his company. Now he began to worry. How long was Ben going to stay? He was sure to find out soon that Matt was living alone. When he did, would he decide it was more comfortable here than in an Indian village? At the rate he had wolfed down that supper, the flour and molasses wouldn't hold out long. Would he expect Matt to go on providing meals and waiting on him?

And why had he left that town on the river in such a hurry? Was there really some charge against him? Was he dangerous — perhaps even a murderer? At the thought, Matt sat up on his pine bed. He'd be sensible to stay awake and on guard. He'd half a mind to fetch down his father's rifle and keep it near at hand. Then he felt ashamed. What would his father say about begrudging a stranger a meal and a night's rest? All the same, he was determined not to shut his eyes that night.

He kept them open for a long time, but suddenly he jerked out of a deep sleep and saw that daylight was streaming across the cabin floor. The cabin door was open, and the man was gone.

Perhaps he had only stepped outside. Matt stumbled to the door. No sign of the stranger. Relief flooded over him. All that worrying, and the man had never intended to stay. Perhaps he had actually believed the lie that his father was returning that day. Then once again, Matt felt ashamed. He must have made it only too plain that Ben wasn't welcome. Would Pa say he had done wrong?

Still, it was too early to be sure. At any moment Ben might appear, hungry for breakfast. He had better stir up some fresh corn cake.

It was then that he noticed. His father's rifle was not hanging over the door. In a panic, he searched the cabin, his own bed, the corner shelves, under the table and the stools. He rushed back to the door and on to the edge of the forest. It was no use. No way of telling which way the man had taken or how long he had been on his way while Matt slept. Ben was gone, and so was the rifle.

He should have kept it in his hands, as his hunch had warned him. He could see now that the man had had his mind set on that gun from the moment he laid eyes on it. But even if Matt had had it in his hands, could he have held out against those burly arms? And to keep his gun, could he actually have shot a man — even a criminal?

It was only later, when his rage began to die down, that he felt a prickle of fear. Now he had no protection. And no way to get meat. Sick with anger, he sat staring at his row of notched sticks. It would be a month at least before his father returned. A month of nothing but fish! And what would his father say?

CHAPTER 4

IT WAS HARD TO BE DEPRIVED OF THE HUNTING.
Now whenever he went into the forest, the squirrels
and the rabbits frisked about boldly, knowing perfectly
well he had no gun in his hands. Once, he was certain
he could have had a good shot at a deer. Instead, he
went fishing, and he knew he ought to be grateful that
the creek and the pond could provide all the food he
needed, even though fish didn't seem to stick to his ribs
like a good meat stew. Here and there in a sunny spot
he discovered a patch of blueberries. Gradually his
spirits rose again. The July weather was perfect. The
flies and mosquitoes were less bothersome. He began
to count the days ahead instead of the ones he had
notched. Two or three more sticks and his family
would be here. The corn was growing taller. The little
hard green pumpkins were rounding out. He could
wait a little longer.

Perhaps he even became a mite careless.

He had been fishing all one morning. A good, clear
day, the water still nippy on his ankles, the sun warm
on his bare head. He had followed the creek a long way
and had a lucky catch. He came whistling out of the
woods, swinging four speckled trout. He quieted down

of a sudden when he heard a crackling in the underbrush close by. Then he stopped short at sight of the cabin. The door was swinging open at a crazy angle, one hinge broken. Across the doorsill some white stuff dribbled, like spilled flour.

With a shout, he dropped the fish and ran. It *was* flour! Tracked all over the cabin floor, the sack ripped open and dragged across the room. The cabin was a shambles, the stools overturned, the shelf swept bare, the precious molasses keg upside down on the floor and empty.

Ben must have come back! For a moment hot sparks of anger drove every sensible thought out of his head. Then he knew it couldn't have been Ben. Ben was too fond of food to waste it. Indians? No, it wasn't possible any human being would scatter food about like this. With a sinking heart he realized what had happened. He remembered the thrashing in the underbrush. It had to be a bear. Somehow he had neglected to bar the door securely.

Well, the damage was done, and the bear would be half a mile away by now. Helpless with fury at his own carelessness, he stood for some time in the middle of the cabin, unable to pull his wits together. Then he went down on his hands and knees and carefully began to scrape up the traces of flour. After a time he gave up. The best he had managed to salvage was two handfuls of gritty, unappetizing meal, even though he took the good pewter spoon and dug into the hollows of the dirt floor.

After a long time he felt hungry enough to remember the fish. Halfheartedly he cleaned them, and blew up the fire and roasted them. He found a few grains of salt left in the tin to sprinkle on them. He would have to make the best of it. He wouldn't starve as long as he had a fishline. But tomorrow he would not even have salt.

CHAPTER 5

DAY AFTER DAY HE KEPT REMEMBERING THE BEE TREE. He and his father had discovered it weeks ago. High in a tree, at the swampy edge of the pond they had called Loon Pond, the bees were buzzing in and out of an old woodpecker hole. Matt had thought they were wild bees, but his father said no, there were no bees at all in America till the colonists brought them from England. This swarm must have escaped from one of the river towns. Bees were better left alone, Pa said.

He felt he could scarcely endure another meal of plain fish. He was hungry for a bit of something tasty. Knowing so well his fondness for molasses, his mother had persuaded them to carry that little keg all the way to Maine when his father would rather have gone without. She would have smiled to see him running his finger round and round the empty keg like a child and licking off the last drop the bear had missed. Now he couldn't stop thinking about that honey. It would be worth a sting or two just to have a taste of it. There couldn't be much danger in going up that tree and taking just a little — a cupful perhaps that the bees would never miss. One morning he made up his mind to try it, come what might.

It was an easy tree to climb, with branches as neatly placed as the rungs of a ladder. The bees did not seem to notice as he pulled himself higher and higher. Even when his head was on a level with the hole, they flew lazily in and out, not paying him any mind. The hole was small, not big enough for his hand and the spoon he had brought with him. Peering in, he could just glimpse, far inside, the golden mass of honeycomb. The bark all around the hole was rotted and crumbling. Cautiously he put his fingers on the edge and gave a slight tug. A good-sized piece of bark broke off into his hand.

With it came the bees. With a furious buzzing they came pouring from the broken hole. The humming grew to a roar, like a great wind. Matt felt a sharp pain on his neck, then another and another. The angry creatures swarmed along his hands and bare arms, in his hair, on his face.

How he got down out of that tree he never remembered. Water! If he could reach water he could escape them. Bellowing and waving his arms, he plunged toward the pond. The bees were all around him. He could not see through the whirling cloud of them. The boggy ground sucked at his feet. He pulled one foot clear out of his boot, went stumbling over sharp roots to the water's edge, and flung himself forward. His foot caught in a fallen branch and he wrenched it clear. Dazed with pain, he sank down into the icy shelter of the water.

He came up choking. Just above the water the angry bees circled. Twice more he ducked his head and held it down till his lungs were bursting. He tried to swim out into the pond but his feet were tangled in dragging weeds. When he tried to jerk them free, a fierce pain ran up his leg and he went under again, thrashing his arms wildly.

Then something lifted him. His head came up from the water and he gulped air into his aching lungs. He felt strong arms around him. Half conscious, he dreamed that his father was carrying him, and he did not wonder how this could be. Presently he knew he was lying on dry ground. Though his eyelids were swollen almost shut, he could see two figures bending over him — unreal, half-naked figures with dark faces. Then, as his wits began to return to him, he saw that they were Indians, an old man and a boy. The man's hands were reaching for his throat, and in panic Matt tried to jerk away.

"Not move," a deep voice ordered. "Bee needles have poison. Must get out."

Matt was too weak to struggle. He could not even lift his head. Now that he was out of the cold water, his skin seemed to be on fire from head to toe, yet he could not stop shivering. He had to lie helpless while the man's hands moved over his face and neck and body. Gradually he realized that they were gentle hands, probing and rubbing at one tender spot after another. His panic began to die away.

He could still not think clearly. Things seemed to keep fading before he could quite grasp them. He could not protest when the man lifted him again and carried him like a baby. It did not seem to matter where they were taking him, but shortly he found himself lying on his own bed in his own cabin. He was alone; the Indians had gone. He lay, too tired and sore to figure out how he came to be there, knowing only that the nightmare of whirling bees and choking water was past and that he was safe.

Some time passed. Then once again the Indian was bending over him, holding a wooden spoon against his lips. He swallowed in spite of himself, even when he found it was not food, but some bitter medicine. He was left alone again, and presently he slept.

CHAPTER 6

FINALLY MATT WOKE AND KNEW THAT HE WAS WELL.
His body was no longer on fire. He could open his eyes,
and he saw that sunlight glinted through the chinks in
the roof. All his familiar things were around him – the
shelves with the pewter dishes, his jacket hanging on a
peg. He felt as though he had been on a long journey
and had come home. He must have slept through half a
day and a night.

When the cabin door opened and the Indian entered,
Matt hastily pulled himself up. Now, with clear eyes,
he saw that there was nothing in the least strange about
this man. He was dressed not so differently from Matt's
own father, in a coat of some rough brown cloth and
leggings fringed down the side. His face was smooth-
shaven, and so was his whole head, except for one long
black topknot. When he saw that Matt was awake, his
stern face was lighted by a wide smile.

"Good." It was half word, half grunt. "White boy
very sick. Now well."

Matt remembered his father's advice. "Good morning," he said respectfully.

The Indian pointed a hand at his own chest. "Saknis,
family of beaver," he said. He seemed to be waiting.

"I'm Matthew Hallowell," Matt answered.

"Good. White man leave you here?"

"Just for a while," Matt told him. "He has gone to get my mother." It did not occur to him to lie to this old man as he had to Ben. Moreover, he knew that there was something he had to say. He tried to find the right words.

"I'm grateful to you," he said finally. "It was a very lucky thing you happened to find me."

"We watch. White boy very foolish to climb bee tree."

So, he had been right, Matt thought, that eyes were watching him from the forest. He was sure that the Indian had not asked him where he lived. They had brought him straight home to this cabin. Even though he knew it was his good fortune they'd been watching him yesterday, he still felt somewhat resentful of their spying. Abruptly he swung his feet to the floor, and winced as a sharp pain ran up his leg.

The Indian noticed, and moving closer he took Matt's ankle between his hands and pressed gently with his fingers.

"Is it broken?" Matt asked.

"*Nda*. Not broke. Mend soon. Sleep now. Not need medicine more."

The Indian had put something on the table as he came in. When he had gone, Matt hobbled over to see what it was and found a wooden bowl of stew, thick and greasy, flavored with some strange plant, wonderfully filling and strengthening. With it there was a cake of corn bread, coarser than his own but delicious.

The next day the Indian brought the boy with him.

"*Nkweniss*. You call grandson," he announced. "Attean."

The two boys stared at each other. The Indian boy's black eyes held no expression whatever. Unlike the old man, he was naked except for a breechcloth held up by a string at his waist. It passed between his legs and hung down like a little apron back and front. His heavy black hair fell straight to his shoulders.

"Attean same winter as white boy, maybe?" the man asked. He held up ten fingers and then four more.

"I'm thirteen," Matt answered, holding up his own fingers. At least, he excused himself, that would be true in another week.

The Indian boy did not speak a word. Quite plainly he had been brought here against his will. He stared about the cabin and seemed to despise everything he saw. He made Matt feel like a fool, sitting with his leg propped up on a stool. Matt steadied himself on his good leg and stood up.

Now he noticed that Saknis was holding out to him a rough sort of crutch. Matt wished he did not have to try it right now, with both of them watching him, but he could see that the man expected it. He managed a few steps, furious at his own clumsiness. He had never imagined how pesky a crutch could be. Moreover, although there was not the slightest change in the boy's face, Matt was sure that Attean was laughing at him. There was a nasty little gleam in the boy's eyes.

The moment they were gone, he seized the crutch in earnest, and very soon he could swing himself along at a good, brisk pace. Now he was able to get about outside the cabin, to check the corn patch and bring in firewood.

The trouble was, he had only one boot. The woolen stocking his mother had knit for him was wearing thin. On the rough ground it wore through in no time.

This too the Indian noticed, when he came with his grandson next morning. "No boot," he said, pointing.

"I lost it," Matt answered. "It came off in the mud when I ran." Once again he felt ridiculous under the Indian boy's black stare.

Three days later Saknis brought him a pair of moccasins. They were handsome and new, of moosehide, dark and glistening with grease, tied with stout thongs that were long enough to wrap about his ankles.

"Beaver woman make," Saknis said. "Better white man's boots. White boy see."

Matt took off his one boot and slipped on the moccasins. Indeed they were better! In fact they were wonderful. Not stiff like new leather boots. Not knobby or pinching anywhere. Light as nothing at all when he lifted his feet. No wonder Indians did not make a sound when they walked in the forest.

Shame suddenly flooded over Matt. This man had perhaps saved his life, had come bringing food and a crutch, and now these beautiful moccasins. It wasn't enough just to say an awkward thank you. He needed to give something in return. Not money. There were a few silver coins in the tin box, but something made him very sure that he could not offer money to this proud old man. He looked about him in despair. There was almost nothing of his own in the cabin.

Then he spied the two books on the shelf, the only two his father had been able to carry into the wilderness.

One was the Bible. He dared not give away his father's Bible. The other book was his own, the only one he had ever possessed. *Robinson Crusoe*. He had read it a dozen times and the thought of parting with it was painful, but it was the only thing he had to give. He hobbled across the room and took it down from the shelf and held it out to the Indian.

Saknis stared at it.

"It's for you," Matt said. "It's a gift. Please take it."

Saknis reached out and took the book in his hand. He turned it over and over slowly, his face showing not a sign of pleasure. Then he opened it and stood peering at the page. With shame, Matt saw that he was holding it upside down.

He couldn't read. Of course he couldn't. Matt should have known that. He had made a terrible mistake and embarrassed the good man. He had heard once that the one thing an Indian could never forgive was a hurt to his pride. He felt his own face burning.

But Saknis did not look embarrassed. His dark stare went from the book to Matt's face.

"White boy know signs?" he asked.

Matt was puzzled.

"White boy read what white man write here?"

"Yes," Matt admitted. "I can read it."

For a long moment the Indian studied the book. Then, astonishingly, that rare white smile flashed.

"Good," he grunted. "Saknis make treaty."

"A treaty?" Matt was even more puzzled.

"*Nkweniss* hunt. Bring white boy bird and rabbit. White boy teach Attean white man's signs."

"You mean — I should teach him to read?"

"Good. White boy teach Attean what book say."

Doubtfully, Matt looked from the old man to the boy, who stood silently listening. His heart sank. The scorn in the boy's face had turned to black anger.

"*Nda!*" The furious word exploded, the first word Matt had ever heard him speak. Half under his breath he muttered a string of incomprehensible words.

His grandfather's stern face did not change. He was undisturbed by the boy's defiance.

"Attean learn," he said. "White man come more and more to Indian land. White man not make treaty with pipe. White man make signs on paper, signs Indian not know. Indian put mark on paper to show him friend of white man. Then white man take land. Tell Indian cannot hunt on land. Attean learn to read white man's signs. Attean not give away hunting grounds."

The boy glowered at his grandfather, but he did not dare to speak again. With a black scowl, he stalked out of the cabin.

"Good," said Saknis calmly. He handed the book back to Matt. "Attean come *seba* — tomorrow."

CHAPTER 7

BEFORE HE HAD HIS EYES OPEN NEXT MORNING, Matt knew that something was wrong with this day. When it came back to him he sat up with a groan. Attean! What had possessed him to give a book to an Indian? How could he possibly teach a savage to read?

He tried to think back to the time his mother had taught him his ABCs. He could plainly see that brown-covered primer she held in her hands. He had detested it. He had had to learn the short verses printed beside each letter.

> A In Adam's fall
>   We sinned all.

That would hardly do. To be honest, he wasn't sure to this day just what it meant. He would feel mighty silly trying to explain it to a heathen. Then happily he recalled another book that had been sent to his sister, Sarah, from England, with a small picture to illustrate each letter. No nonsense about Adam. *A* was for *apple*. Sarah had been luckier than he.

But he had no way of making pictures, and there were no apples here in the forest. What could he find for *A* that an Indian would understand? He looked about the cabin. *T* for *table*, though it was unlikely they'd ever get as far as *T*. How about *A* for *arm*? That was simple enough. *B*? His eye fell on the leg bone of the squirrel left from last night's meal. The stub of a candle would do for *C*. *D*? *Door* would be just the word for Attean. He certainly could walk out of one fast enough, and would again, no doubt, long before they got to *D*.

He doubted that Attean would come. Still, he had better be ready. He stirred the fire, ate a chunk of the cold Indian corn cake, and set about to prepare a schoolroom. He shoved the two stools together and laid *Robinson Crusoe* on the table. He did not have paper or ink. He found a ribbon of birchbark in a corner and tore off a strip and sharpened a stick to a point. Then he waited.

Attean came, swinging a dead rabbit by the ears. He slung it disdainfully on the table.

"Thank you," Matt said. "That's a big one. I won't need anything else for several days."

His politeness brought no response.

"Sit here," he ordered. He hesitated. "I never thought as how I'd have to teach anyone to read. But I have figured a way to start."

Silently the boy sat down, as straight and rigid as a cedar post. When Matt hunched himself onto the other stool, the boy's scowl deepened. Plainly he did not like having the white boy so close to him. Attean had no need to be finicky, Matt thought. He smelled none too sweet himself. The grease smeared on his body, even

33

on his hair, stunk up the whole cabin. It was supposed to keep off the mosquitoes, he'd heard, but he thought he'd rather have the pesky insects himself. He drew a letter on the birch bark.

"This is the first letter," he explained. "*A*. *A* for *arm*."

He repeated this several times, pointing to his own arm. Attean kept to his stubborn, scornful silence. Matt set his jaw. He could be stubborn too, he decided. He opened *Robinson Crusoe*.

"We'll pick out the *A*'s on this page," he said, trying to control his impatience. He pointed. "Now you show me one."

Attean stared straight ahead of him in silence. Then, to Matt's astonishment, he grudgingly laid a grubby finger on a letter *A*.

"Good," said Matt, copying the word Saknis used so often. "Find another."

Suddenly the boy broke his silence. "White man's book foolish," he scoffed. "Write *arm*, *arm*, *arm* all over paper."

Puzzled at first, Matt saw his own mistake. "Hundreds of other words begin with *A*," he explained. "Or have *A* in them. And there are twenty-five more letters."

Attean scowled. "How long?" he demanded.

"What do you mean?"

"How long Attean learn signs in book?"

"It will take some time," Matt said. "There are a lot of long words in this book."

"One moon?"

"One month? Of course not. It might take a year."

With one swift jerk of his arm, Attean knocked the

book from the table. Before Matt could speak, he was out of the cabin and gone.

"Reckon that's the end of the lessons," Matt said to himself. Cheerfully he began to skin the rabbit.

CHAPTER 8

BY THE NEXT MORNING HE WAS HALF SORRY THE BOY
would not be coming again. He didn't know whether he
was annoyed or relieved when Attean walked through
the door without a sign of greeting and sat down at the
table.

Matt decided to skip *B* for *bone*. In the night he had
thought of a better way.

"This book isn't a treaty," he began. "It's a story. It's
about a man who gets shipwrecked on a desert island.
I'll read some of it out loud to show you."

He opened *Robinson Crusoe* at the first page and began
to read.

> *I was born in the year 1632,*
> *in the city of York. . . .*

He stopped. He remembered suddenly how the first
time he had tried to read this book he had found that
first page so dull he had come close to giving up right
there. He had better skip the beginning and get on
with the story if he wanted to catch Attean's attention.

"I'll read the part about the storm at sea," he said.

He had read the book so many times that he knew
exactly where to find the right page. Taking a deep

breath, as though he were struggling in the water himself, he chose the page where Robinson Crusoe was dashed from the lifeboat and swallowed up in the sea.

Nothing can describe the confusion of thought which I felt when I sunk into the water, for though I swam very well, yet I could not deliver myself from the waves so as to draw breath . . . for I saw the sea come after me as high as a great hill, and as furious as an enemy. . . .

Matt looked up from the page. There was not a flicker of interest in the boy's face. Had he understood a single word? Discouraged, he laid down the book. What did a storm at sea mean to a savage who had lived all his life in the forest?

"Well," he said lamely, "it gets better as you go along."

Once more Attean took him by surprise. "White man get out of water?" he asked.

"Oh yes," Matt said, delighted. "Everyone else on the ship is drowned. He gets thrown up all alone on an island."

The Indian nodded. He seemed satisfied.

"Shall I read more of it?"

Attean nodded again. "Go now," he said. Come back *seba*."

The next morning there was no question of *B* for *bone*. Matt had the book open and waiting at the part he wanted to read.

"This is about the morning after the storm," he explained. "Robinson Crusoe looks out and sees that part of the ship hasn't sunk yet. He swims out and manages to save some things and carry them to shore." He began to read.

Once again it was impossible to tell whether Attean understood. Presently Matt slowed down. It was discouraging, reading to a wooden post. But Attean spoke at once.

"White man not smart like Indian," he said scornfully. "Indian not need thing from ship. Indian make all thing he need."

Disappointed and cross, Matt put the book down. They might as well get on with the alphabet. He drew a *B* on the birchbark.

After Attean had gone, Matt kept thinking about Robinson Crusoe and all the useful things he had managed to salvage from that ship. He had found a carpenter's chest, for instance. Bags of nails. Two barrels of bullets. And a dozen hatchets – a dozen! Why, Matt and his father had come up here to Maine with one axe and an adz. They had cut down trees and built this whole cabin and the table and the stools without a single nail. Crusoe had found a hammock to sleep in instead of prickly hemlock boughs. He could see now how it must have sounded to Attean. Come to think of it, Robinson Crusoe had lived like a king on that desert island!

❦ CHAPTER 9 ❧

A FEW MORNINGS LATER, AT THE END OF THE LESSON, Matt delayed Attean.

"How did you kill that rabbit?" he asked, pointing to the offering Attean had thrown on the table. "There's no bullet hole in it."

"Indian not use bullet for rabbit," Attean answered scornfully.

"Then how? There's no hole at all."

For a moment it seemed that Attean would not bother to answer. Then the Indian shrugged. "Attean show," he said. "Come."

Matt was dumfounded. It was the first sign the Indian had given of — well, of what exactly? He had not sounded friendly. But there was not time to puzzle this out right now. Attean was walking across the clearing, and he apparently expected Matt to follow. Pleased and curious, Matt hobbled after him, grateful that he no longer needed the crutch.

At the edge of the clearing the Indian stopped and searched the ground. Presently he stooped down under a black spruce tree, poked into the dirt, and jerked up a long, snakelike root. He drew from the leather pouch at his belt a curious sort of knife, the blade curved into a hook. With one sure stroke, he split one end of the root, then peeled off the bark by pulling at it with his teeth. He separated the whole length into two strands, which he spliced together by rolling them against his bare thigh. Next he searched about in the bushes till he found two forked saplings about three feet apart. He trimmed the twigs from these, drawing his knife toward his chest as Matt had been taught not to do. Then he cut a stout branch, and rested it lightly across the forks of his saplings. From the threadlike root he made a noose and suspended it from the stick so that it hung just above the ground. He worked without speaking, and it seemed to Matt that all this took him no time at all.

"Rabbit run into trap," he said finally. "Pull stick into bush, so white boy can kill."

"Golly," said Matt, filled with admiration. "I hadn't thought of making a snare. I didn't know you could make one without string or wire."

"Make more," Attean ordered, pointing into the woods. "Not too close."

After Attean had gone, Matt managed to make two more snares. They were clumsy things, and he was not too proud of them. Splitting a slippery root, he discovered, was not so easy as it had looked. He spoiled a number of them before he mastered the trick of splicing them together. They did not slide as easily as the one Attean had made, but they seemed strong enough.

Next morning he showed his traps to Attean. He had hoped for some sign of approval, but all he got was a grunt and a shrug. He knew that to Attean his work must look childish. However, on the third day one of his own snares had been upset, though the animal had got away. The day after that, to his joy, there was actually a partridge struggling to free itself in the bushes where the stick had caught. This time the grunt with which Attean rewarded him sounded very much like his grandfather's "Good." Silently the Indian watched as Matt reset the snare. Then they walked back to the cabin, Matt swinging his catch as nonchalantly as he had seen Attean do.

"You don't need to bring me any more food," he boasted. "I'll catch my own meat from now on."

Nevertheless, Attean continued to bring him some offering every morning. Not always fresh meat. He seemed to know exactly when Matt had finished the last scrap of rabbit or duck. Sometimes he brought a slab of corn cake, or a pouch full of nuts, once a small cake of maple sugar. Plainly he felt bound to keep the terms of his grandfather's treaty.

Matt stuck to his part of the bargain as well, though the lessons were an ordeal for them both. Matt knew well enough what a poor teacher he was. Sometimes it seemed that Attean was learning in spite of him. Once the Indian had resigned himself to mastering twenty-six letters, he took them in a gulp, scorning the childish *candle* and *door* and *table* that Matt had devised. Soon he was spelling out simple words. The real trouble was that Attean was contemptuous, that the whole matter of white man's words seemed to him nonsense. Impatiently they hurried through the lessons to get on with *Robinson*

41

Crusoe. Matt suspected that the only reason Attean agreed to come back day after day was that he wanted to hear more of that story.

Skipping over the pages that sounded like sermons, Matt chose the sections he liked best himself. Now he came to the rescue of the man Friday. Attean sat quietly, and Matt almost forgot him in his own enjoyment of his favorite scene.

There was the mysterious footprint on the sand, the canoes drawn up on the lonely beach, and the strange, wild-looking men with two captives. One of the captives they mercilessly slaughtered. The fire was set blazing for a cannibal feast.

Then the second captive made a desperate escape, running straight to where Crusoe stood watching. Two savages pursued him with horrid yells. Matt glanced up from the book and saw that Attean's eyes were gleaming. He hurried on. No need to skip here. Crusoe struck a mighty blow at the first cannibal, knocking him senseless. Then, seeing that the other was fitting an arrow into his bow, he shot and killed him. Matt read on:

> *The poor savage who fled, but had stopped, though he saw both his enemies had fallen . . . yet was so frightened with the noise and fire of my piece, that he stood stock-still, and neither came forward nor went backward. . . . I hallooed again to him, and made signs to him to come forward, which he easily understood, and came a*

42

little way, then stopped again. . . . he
stood trembling as if he had been taken
prisoner, and just been to be killed, as
his two enemies were. I beckoned to him
again to come to me, and gave him all
signs of encouragement, that I could
think of; and he came nearer and nearer,
kneeling down every ten or twelve steps,
in token of acknowledgment for saving
his life. I smiled at him, and looked
pleasantly, and beckoned to him to come
still nearer. At length he came close to
me, and then he kneeled down again,
kissed the ground, and, taking my foot,
set it upon his head. This, it seemed,
was a token of swearing to be my slave
forever. . . .

Attean sprang to his feet, a thundercloud wiping out all pleasure from his face.

"*Nda!*" he shouted. "Not so."

Matt stopped, bewildered.

"Him never do that!"

"Never do what?"

"Never kneel down to white man!"

"But Crusoe had saved his life."

"Not kneel down," Attean repeated fiercely. "Not be slave. Better die."

Matt opened his mouth to protest, but Attean gave him no chance. In three steps he was out of the cabin.

Now he'll never come back, Matt thought. He sat

slowly turning over the pages. He had never questioned that story. Like Robinson Crusoe, he had thought it natural and right that the wild man should be the white man's slave. Was there perhaps another possibility? The thought was new and troubling.

~CHAPTER 10~

HE FELT WEAK WITH RELIEF WHEN NEXT MORNING
Attean walked stiffly into the cabin and sat down at the
table. Stumbling over himself, he set about the lesson.
As soon as he could, he picked up *Robinson Crusoe*. In
the night he had carefully thought out just what he was
going to say, if Attean ever gave him another chance.
Now he had to talk fast, because he could see that
Attean was set against hearing any more of this book.

"Let me go on," he pleaded. "It's different from now
on. Friday — that's what Robinson Crusoe named him —
doesn't kneel anymore."

"Not slave?"

"No," Matt lied. "After that they get to be — well —
companions. They share everything together."

Ignoring the suspicion on Attean's face, Matt began
hurriedly to read. He was thankful that he knew the
book so well that he was able to see when trouble might
be coming. One of the first words Crusoe taught his
man Friday was the word *master*. Luckily he caught
that one in time. And it was true, Crusoe and his new
companion did go about together, sharing their adventures. Only, Matt thought, it would have been better
perhaps if Friday hadn't been quite so thickheaded.

After all, there must have been a thing or two about that desert island that a native who had lived there all his life could have taught Robinson Crusoe.

When Matt closed the book, Attean nodded. Then, as so many times before, he took Matt by surprise.

"You like go fish?" he asked.

"I sure would," Matt said gratefully.

Stopping to pick up his fish pole from beside the door, he ran to overtake the Indian boy, who strode ahead. He knew his grin was stretching from one ear to the other, but he couldn't hide his feelings as Attean did.

They walked some distance, Matt managing to keep pace with the Indian's swift stride, determined not to let Attean know that his ankle was aching. They seemed to be following no particular trail. Finally they came out on a part of the creek that Matt had not seen before. It was shallow here, studded with rocks and pebbles, so that the water, rippling over them, made little rapids or collected in quiet pools. Here Attean stopped, broke off a sapling, and instead of making a fish pole, drew his knife from his pouch and quickly shaved a sharp point, making a spear. Then he stepped gently into the stream. Matt stood watching.

Attean stood motionless, peering intently into a pool of clear water. All at once he stooped, darted his spear with one quick stroke, and came up with a glittering fish. He studied it for a moment. "Too small," he decided. To Matt's astonishment he spoke to the fish quite solemnly, a few incomprehensible words, then tossed it back into the stream. In a few moments he had speared another, which he judged large enough to keep.

"Do same," he ordered now, coming back to the bank. He handed Matt the spear.

He would just look ridiculous, Matt knew before he started. He waded in and stood up to his knees, looking down into the sliding water. Presently a fish darted past. At least he thought it was a fish. It was hard to tell which was shadow and which might be a fish. At any rate, it was gone before he got his spear into the water. Presently he saw another, this one quite definitely a fish, calmly drifting in the pool. He jabbed at it hopelessly. He was sure his stick actually touched the slippery thing. He lunged at it, lost his footing, and went down with a splash that would scare off any fish for miles around. When he came up dripping, he saw Attean watching him with a horrid grin.

Suddenly he felt hot, in spite of the icy water. Why had Attean brought him out here, anyway? Had Attean just wanted to show off his own cleverness, and to make Matt look more clumsy than ever? Was this Attean's answer, in case Matt had any idea in his head about being a Robinson Crusoe? For a moment Matt glared back at Attean with a scowl as black as any Indian's. Then he wiped his nose with the back of his hand and sloshed back to the bank. He snatched up his own pole and line. He poked about under the wet leaves and found a good, juicy worm and fitted it to his hook.

"I'll do it my own way," he said. "I can catch plenty of fish with this, and that's what matters."

Attean sat on the bank and watched. To Matt's satisfaction, in no time there was a tug on the line, a strong one. An impressive-looking fish rose to the

47

surface, thrashing fiercely. Matt gave a jerk, and the line came swinging out of the water so suddenly that he almost lost his footing again. It was empty.

"Fish broke line," Attean observed.

As if anyone couldn't see that! Furious at Attean, at the fish, and at himself, Matt examined the break, unable to face the Indian. He had lost more than a good fish. His hook had disappeared as well. The only hook he had.

Of course Attean noticed. Those black eyes never missed anything. "Make new hook," he suggested.

Without even getting to his feet, he reached out and broke a twig off a maple sapling. Out came the crooked knife again. In a few strokes he cut a piece as long as his little finger, carved a groove around the middle, and whittled both ends into sharp points. Now he stepped into the water and tied Matt's line expertly around the groove.

"Put on two worms," he said. "Cover up all hook."

He didn't offer to find the worms. Matt had lost all interest in fishing. He knew that somehow or other he would just provide more amusement for Attean. But he couldn't refuse.

He didn't have to wait long before another fish caught hold. This time he landed it neatly.

"Good," said Attean from the bank. "Big."

Matt was trying to get it off the line. "He swallowed the whole hook," he said.

"Better white man's hook," Attean said. "Turn around inside fish. Not get away."

Back on the bank Matt slit the fish and extracted the hook and his line. But the thin twig had broken in half.

"Easy make new hook," Attean said. "Make many hooks."

Of course. Looking down at the simple thing in his hand, Matt realized that he never again need worry about losing a hook. He could make a new one wherever he happened to be. It was another necessary thing that Attean had shown him, just as he had made the snare. He wasn't sure why Attean had bothered. But grudgingly he had to admit that Attean had proved to him once again that he didn't always have to depend on white man's tools.

All at once he was hungry. The sun was straight overhead, and it would be a long tramp back through the woods before he could cook his fish. Now he saw that Attean had the same thought.

The Indian was heaping up a small pile of pine needles and grass. He drew from his muskrat-skin pouch a piece of hard stone with bits of quartz embedded in it. Striking it with his knife, he soon had a spark, which he blew into a flame.

I could have done that myself, Matt thought. In fact he had done it many a time, but he had not realized that he could use a common stone as well as his flint.

"Get fish ready," Attean ordered now, pointing to the two fish on the bank. Matt did not like his masterful tone, but he did as he was told. By the time he had the two fish split and gutted and washed in the creek, Attean had a fire blazing. Matt was curious to see how he would go about the cooking.

He watched as Attean cut two short branches, bending

49

them first to make sure they were green. He trimmed and sharpened them rapidly. Then he thrust a pointed end into each fish from head to tail. A small green stick was set crosswise inside the fish to hold the sides apart. He handed one stick to Matt. One on each side of the fire, the two boys squatted and held their sticks to the blaze. From time to time Attean fed the fire with dry twigs. When the flesh was crisp and brown, they ate, still silently.

Matt licked his fingers. His resentment had vanished along with his hunger. "Golly," he said, "that was the best fish I ever ate."

"Good," said Attean. Across the fire he looked at Matt, and his eyes gleamed. He was laughing again, but somehow not with scorn.

"What did you say to that fish you threw back?" Matt was still curious.

"I say to him not to tell other fish," Attean said seriously. "Not scare away."

"You actually think a fish could understand?"

Attean shrugged. "Fish know many thing," he replied.

Matt sat pondering this strange idea. "Well, it seemed to work," he said finally. "At least the other fish came along."

A wide grin spread slowly across Attean's face. It was the first time Matt had seen him smile.

CHAPTER 11

ONE MORNING MATT LAID HIS STICKS IN A ROW. Seven sticks, each with seven notches. That meant that it was well into August. The silk tassels were glistening on the cornstalks. The hard green pumpkins nestling underneath the stalks were rounding out and taking on a coating of orange. It was time for his father to be coming. At any moment he might look out and see him walking into the clearing, bringing his mother and Sarah and the new baby. It was strange to think there was a member of the family he had never seen. Was it a boy or a girl? It would be a fine thing to have them sitting around the table again.

He hoped his mother would take over the reading lessons, which were going badly. Attean still came almost every day, though there was no longer any need for him to bring meat or fish. Matt couldn't make out why the Indian kept coming since he made it so plain he disliked the lessons. So often Attean made him feel uncomfortable and ridiculous. But he had to admit that on the days when Attean did not come the hours went by slowly.

Often Attean seemed in no hurry to leave when the morning's lesson was over. "Look see if catch rabbit," he might suggest, and together they would go out to check the snares. Or they would tramp along the creek to a good spot for fishing. Attean seemed to have plenty of time on his hands. Sometimes he would just hang around and watch Matt do the chores. He would stand at the edge of the corn patch and look on while Matt pulled up weeds.

"Squaw work," he commented once.

Matt flushed. "We think it's a man's work," he retorted.

Attean said nothing. He did not offer to help. After a time he just wandered off without saying goodbye. It must be mighty pleasant, Matt thought to himself, to just hunt and fish all day long and not have any work to do. That wasn't his father's way, and it wouldn't ever be his. The work was always waiting to be done, but if he got the corn patch cleared and the wood chopped today, he could go fishing with Attean tomorrow — if Attean invited him.

Sometimes Attean brought an old dog with him. It was about the sorriest-looking hound Matt had ever seen, with a coat of coarse brown hair, a mangy tail, and whitish patches on its face that gave it a clownish look. Its long pointed nose was misshapen with bumps and bristles. By the look of its ears, it had survived many battles. The instant it spied Matt, a ridge of hair went straight up on its back and it let out a mean growl. Attean cuffed it sharply, and after that it was quiet, but it watched the white stranger with wary eyes and kept its distance.

Matt tried not to show his own distrust. "What's his name?" he asked politely.

Attean shrugged. "No name. *Aremus* – dog."

"If he doesn't have a name, how can he come when you call?"

"Him my dog. Him come."

As though he knew what Attean had said, the scruffy tail began to weave back and forth.

"*Piz wat*," Attean said. "Good for nothing. No good for hunt. No sense. Him fight anything – bear, moose." There was no mistaking the pride in Attean's voice.

"What's wrong with his nose?"

Attean grinned. "Him fight anything. Chase *kogw* – what white man call? Needles all over."

"Oh – a porcupine. Golly, that must have hurt."

"Pull out many needle. Some very deep, not come out. Dog not feel them now."

Maybe not, Matt thought, but he doubted those quills had improved the dog's disposition. He didn't fancy this dog of Attean's.

During the lesson the dog prowled about outside the cabin and finally thumped down on the path to bite and scratch at fleas. When Attean came out, the dog leaped up, prancing and yapping as though Attean had been gone for days. Matt thought a little better of him for that. It minded him how his father's dog had made a fuss every time his father came home. That old hound must have just about wagged its tail off when his father came back from Maine. The fact was, Matt was a little jealous of Attean. A dog would be mighty fine company here in the woods, no matter how scrawny it looked.

But not this one. No matter how often the dog came

with Attean, he never let Matt touch him. Nor did Matt like him any better. He was certainly no good at hunting. When the two boys walked through the woods the dog zigzagged ahead, sending squirrels racing up trees and jays chattering, and ruining any chance of a catch. Matt wondered why Attean wanted him along. Attean didn't pay him any mind except to shout at him and cuff him when he was too noisy. But for all his show of indifference, it was plain to Matt that Attean thought a sight of that dog.

Attean had not brought the dog with him the day that he led Matt a long distance into a part of the forest that Matt had never seen. Following after him, Matt began to feel uneasy. If Attean should take himself off suddenly, as he had a way of doing, Matt was not sure he could find his way back to the cabin. It occurred to him that Attean knew this, that perhaps Attean had brought him so far just to show him how helpless he really was, how all the words in a white man's book were of no use to him in the woods.

Yet he did not think this would happen. For some reason he could not explain to himself, he trusted Attean. He didn't really like him. When the Indian got that disdainful look in his eyes, Matt hated him. But somehow, as they had sat side by side, day after day, doing the lessons that neither of them wanted to do, something had changed. Perhaps it had been *Robinson Crusoe*, or the tramping through the woods together. They didn't like each other, but they were no longer enemies.

When they came upon a row of short tree stumps,

birch and aspen cut off close to the ground, Matt's heart gave a leap. Were there settlers nearby? Or Indians? There was no proper clearing. Then he noticed that whoever had cut the trees had left jagged points on each one. No axe would cut a tree in that way. He could see marks where the trees had been dragged along the ground.

In a few steps the boys came out on the bank of an unfamiliar creek. There Matt saw what had happened to those trees. They had been piled in a mound right over the water, from one bank to the other. Water trickled through them in tiny cascades. Behind the piled-up branches, a small pond stretched smooth and still.

"It's a beaver dam!" he exclaimed. "The first one I've ever seen."

"*Qwa bit*," said Attean. "Have red tail. There beaver wigwam." He pointed to a heap of branches at one side, some of them new with green leaves still clinging. Matt stepped closer to look. Instantly there was the crack of a rifle. A ring of water rippled the surface of the pond. Near its edge a black head appeared for just a flash and vanished again in a splutter of bubbles.

Attean laughed at the way Matt had started. "Beaver make big noise with tail," he explained.

"I thought someone had shot a gun," Matt said. "I wish I had my rifle now."

Attean scowled. "Not shoot," he warned. "Not white man, not Indian. Young beaver not ready."

He pointed to a tree nearby. "Sign of beaver," he said. "Belong to family."

Carved on the bark, Matt could make out the crude figure of an animal that could, with some imagination, be a beaver.

"Sign show beaver house belong to people of beaver," Attean explained. "By and by, when young beaver all grown, people of beaver hunt here. No one hunt but people of beaver."

"You mean, just from that mark on the tree, another hunter would not shoot here?"

"That our way," Attean said gravely. "All Indian understand."

Would a white man understand? Matt wondered. He thought of Ben with his stolen rifle. It wasn't likely Ben would respect an Indian sign. But he must remember to warn his father.

When it seemed the beaver did not intend to show itself again, the two boys climbed back up the bank. At the row of stumps, Attean halted and signaled for Matt to go ahead.

"Show way to cabin," he ordered.

All Matt's suspicions came rushing back. Did Attean intend to sneak off behind his back and leave him to find his own way home?

"Is this some kind of trick?" he demanded hotly.

Attean looked stern. "Not trick," he said. "Matt need learn."

To Matt's relief, he took the lead again. After a short distance he stopped and pointed to a broken stick leaning in the direction of the creek. A little farther on there was a small stone set against a larger one. Not far away a tuft of dried grass dangled from a branch of a small tree.

"Indian make sign," Attean said. "Always make sign to tell way. Matt must same. Not get lost in forest."

Now Matt remembered how Attean had paused every so often, sometimes to break off a branch that hung in their path, once to nudge aside a stone with the toe of his moccasin. He had done these things so quickly that Matt had paid no mind. He saw now that Attean had carefully been leaving markers.

"Of course," he exclaimed. "But my father always made blazes on the trees with his knife."

Attean nodded. "That white man's way. Indian maybe not want to show where he go. Not want hunters to find beaver house."

So these were secret signs. Nothing anyone following them would notice. It would take sharp eyes to find them, even if you knew they were there.

"Matt do same," Attean repeated. "Always make sign to show way back."

Matt was ashamed of his suspicions. Attean had only meant to help him. If only he didn't have to be so superior about it.

He plodded along behind Attean, trying to spot the signs before Attean could point them out. All at once, as a thought struck him, he almost laughed out loud. He remembered Robinson Crusoe and his man Friday. He and Attean had sure enough turned that story right round about. Whenever they went a few steps from the cabin, it was the brown savage who strode ahead, leading the way, knowing just what to do and doing it quickly and skillfully. And Matt, a puny sort of Robinson Crusoe, tagged along behind, grateful for the smallest sign that he could do anything right.

It wasn't that he wanted to be a master. And the idea of Attean's being anyone's slave was not to be thought of. He just wished he could make Attean think a little better of him. He wanted Attean to look at him without that gleam of amusement in his eyes. He wished that it were possible for him to win Attean's respect.

As though Attean sensed that Matt was disgruntled, he stopped, whipped out his knife, and neatly sliced off two shining gobs of dried sap from a nearby spruce. He grinned and held out one of them like a peace offering. "Chaw," he ordered. He popped the other piece into his mouth and began to chew with evident pleasure.

Gingerly, Matt copied him. The gob fell to pieces between his teeth, filling his mouth with a bitter juice. He wanted to spit it out in disgust, but Attean was plainly enjoying the stuff, so he stubbornly forced his jaws to keep moving. In a moment the bits came together in a rubbery gum, and the first bitterness gave way to a fresh piney taste. To his surprise, it was very good. The two boys tramped on, chewing companionably. Once more, Matt acknowledged to himself, Attean had taught him another secret of the forest.

ᗍ CHAPTER 12 ᗎ

I MUST HAVE A BOW, MATT DECIDED ONE MORNING. He was envious of the bow Attean often carried behind his shoulder, and of the blunt arrows he tucked into his belt. Only the day before, Matt had watched him swing it suddenly into position and bring down a flying duck. Attean had picked up the dead bird carefully and carried it away with him. No doubt the Indians would find some use for every scrap of bone and feather. Matt knew by now that Attean never shot anything just for the fun of it. With a bow and a little practice, Matt thought now, he might get a duck for himself. It would be a fine change from his usual fish.

He had no doubt he could shoot with a bow. In fact he had made them years ago back in Quincy. He and his friends had played at Indians, stalking each other through the woods and whooping out from behind trees. They had even practiced half-earnestly at shooting at a target. How could he have known that someday he would have need of such a skill?

He cut a straight branch, notched it at either end, and stretched tight a bit of string his father had left. Arrows he whittled out of slender twigs. But something was definitely wrong. His arrows wobbled off in old directions or flopped on the ground a few feet away. He was chagrined when next morning Attean came walking out of the woods and surprised him at his practice.

Attean looked at the bow. "Not good wood," he said at once. "I get better."

He was very exacting about the wood he chose. He searched along the edge of the clearing, testing saplings, bending slender branches, discarding one after another, till he found a dead branch of ash about the thickness of his three fingers. He cut a rod almost his own height and handed it to Matt.

"Take off bark," he directed, and squatted down to watch while Matt scraped the branch clean. Then, taking it in his hands again, he marked off several inches in the center where Matt's hand would grip the bow. "Cut off wood here," he said, running his hand from center to ends. "Make small like this." He held up one slim finger.

Matt set to work too hastily. "Slow," Attean warned him. "Knife take off wood too fast. Indian use stone."

Under the Indian's critical eye, Matt shaved down the branch, paring off the thinnest possible shavings. The slow work took all his patience. Twice he considered the task finished, but Attean, running his hand along the curve of the bow, was not satisfied till it was smooth as an animal bone.

"Need fat now," he said. "Bear fat best."

"Will this do?" Matt asked, bringing out a bowl of fish stew he had left cooling on the table. Carefully, with a bit of bark, Attean skimmed off the drops of oil that had risen to the surface. He rubbed the oil from one end of the bow to the other till the bare wood glistened. Matt's frayed bit of string he cast aside. Instead he set about making a bowstring as he had made the snare, of long strands of spruce root. This took most of the morning as he patiently twisted the strands together, rolling them against his thigh to make them even and smooth.

Finally he tied one end to a notch in the bow and began slowly to bend the wood. The bow seemed to Matt to be as stiff as iron. It seemed impossible that it would bend, but slowly it yielded, till the string slipped over the notch at the other end. The bow was finished.

"It's a beauty," Matt told him, filled with admiration at their joint handiwork.

Attean gave a grunt of satisfaction. "Shoot pretty good," he said. "One day make better. Indian take long time, leave wood many days till ready."

Before he left, Attean cut off four slender shoots of birch wood. "Best for arrow," he explained, marking off with his hands a length of about two feet. He left Matt to do the whittling for himself.

Matt was delighted with the bow, but shooting it was another matter. It was not in the least like the flimsy thing he had first created. It took all his strength to draw back the string. When he released his arrow, it flew with astonishing power off somewhere into the underbrush, anywhere but where he had aimed it. As fast as he could make new arrows he lost them. But he was determined. He pegged a target of birchbark against a tree and shot at it grimly, his arrows coming closer and closer with every day's practice. The heel of his hand was blistered from the stinging snap of the string. Attean did not offer him any further advice, but when the root string began to fray, he brought with him one day a fine bowstring of twisted animal sinew, which would last for a long time. Using the new string, Matt could frequently nick the edge of his target. Soon, he promised himself, the squirrels would have more respect than to frisk about so boldly over his head.

CHAPTER 13

WHEREVER HE WENT NOW, MATT WATCHED FOR Indian signs. Sometimes he could not be sure whether a branch had broken in the wind or whether an animal had scratched a queer-shaped mark on a tree trunk. Once or twice he was certain he had discovered the sign of the beaver. It was a game he played with himself. That it was not a game to Attean he was still to learn. They were following a narrow trail one morning, this time to the east, when Attean halted abruptly.

"Hsst!" he warned.

Off in the brush Matt heard a low, rasping breathing and a frantic scratching in the leaves. The noise stopped the moment they stood still. Moving warily, the boys came upon a fox crouched low on the ground. It did not run, but lay snarling at them, and as he came nearer, Matt saw that its foreleg was caught fast. With a long stick Attean pushed aside the leaves and Matt caught the glint of metal.

"White man's trap," said Attean.

"How do you know?" Matt demanded.

"Indians not use iron trap. Iron trap bad."

"You mean a white man set this trap?" Matt thought of Ben.

"No. Some white man pay for bad Indian to hunt for him. White man not know how to hide trap so good." Attean showed Matt how cleverly the trap had been hidden, the leaves and earth mounded up like an animal burrow with two half-eaten fish heads concealed inside.

The fox watched them, its teeth bared. The angry eyes made Matt uncomfortable. "We're in luck to find it first," he said, to cover his uneasiness.

Attean shook his head. "Not beaver hunting ground," he said. "Turtle clan hunt here." He pointed to a nearby tree. On the bark Matt could just make out a crude scar that had a shape somewhat like a turtle. He was indignant.

"We found it," he said. "You mean you're just going to leave it here because of a mark on a tree?"

"Beaver people not take animal on turtle land," Attean repeated.

"We can't just let it suffer," Matt protested. "Suppose no one comes here for days?"

"Then fox get away."

"How can he get away?"

"Bite off foot."

Indeed, Matt could see now that the creature had already gnawed its own flesh down to the bone. "Leg mend soon," Attean added, noting Matt's troubled face. "Fox have three leg beside."

"I don't like it," Matt insisted. He wondered why he minded so much. He had long ago got used to clubbing the small animals caught in his own snares. There was something about this fox that was different. Those defiant eyes showed no trace of fear. He was struck by the bravery that could inflict such pain on itself to gain freedom. Reluctantly he followed Attean back to the trail, leaving the miserable animal behind.

"It's a cruel way to trap an animal," he muttered. "Worse than our snares."

"*Ehe*," Attean agreed. "My grandfather not allow beaver people to buy iron trap. Some Indian hunt like white man now. One time many moose and beaver. Plenty for all Indians and for white man too. But white man not hunt to eat, only for skin. Him pay Indian to get skin. So Indian use white man's trap."

Matt could not find an answer. Tramping beside Attean he was confused and angry as well. He couldn't understand the Indian code that left an animal to suffer just because of a mark on a tree. And he was fed up with Attean's scorn for white men. It was ridiculous to think that he and Attean could ever really be friends. Sometimes he wished he could never see Attean again.

Even at the same moment, he realized that this was really not true. Even though Attean annoyed him, Matt was constantly goaded to keep trying to win this strange boy's respect. He would lie awake in the night, staring up at the chinks of starlight in the cabin roof, and make up stories in which he himself, not Attean, was the hero. Sometimes he imagined how Attean would be in some terrible danger, and he, Matt, would be brave and calm and come swiftly to the rescue. He would kill a bear unaided, or a panther, or fend off a rattlesnake about to strike. Or he would learn about an enemy band of Indians sneaking through the forest to attack the place where Attean was sleeping, and he would run through the woods and give the alarm in time.

In the morning he laughed at himself for this childish daydreaming. There was little chance he would ever be a hero, and little chance too that Attean would ever need his help. Matt knew that the Indian boy came day after day only because his grandfather sent him. For some reason the old man had taken pity on this helpless white boy, and at the same time he had shrewdly grasped at the chance for his grandson to learn to read. If he suspected that Attean had become the teacher instead, he would doubtless put a stop to the visits altogether.

Matt knew he ought to feel grateful for Attean's teaching. Every day Attean taught him some new thing – a plant like an onion that he could drop into his cooking pot to make his stew more tasty – a weed with a small orange flower and a milky juice in its stem that took away the sting of insect bites or poison ivy – a plant with brownish flowers and roots bearing a string of nutlike bulbs that thickened his stew and made it more nourishing. He had pointed out plants that Matt must never eat, no matter how hungry he might be. He had even shown Matt how to improvise a rain cape in a sudden rain by quickly punching a hole through the center of a wide strip of birchbark and making a cone of bark for his head.

The only thing that Matt could teach him, Attean was set against learning. For Attean the white man's signs on paper were *piz wat* – good for nothing.

Nevertheless, Matt noticed that in spite of himself

Attean had learned something from the white boy. He was speaking the English tongue with greater ease. Perhaps he was not aware himself how differently he spoke. He picked up new words readily. Sometimes he used them with that odd humor that Matt was beginning to recognize. Matt knew that Attean was mocking when some of his own favorite expressions came solemnly out of the Indian's mouth.

"Reckon so," Attean would say. "Rain come soon, by golly." Sometimes he even took a fancy to a word out of *Robinson Crusoe*. He especially liked the sound of *verily*.

In return, Matt liked to try out Indian words. They were not hard to understand but impossible to get his tongue around. He didn't think he could ever quite get them right, but he could see that though it amused Attean when he tried, it also pleased him.

"*Cha kwa* — this morning," Matt might say, "I chased a *kogw* out of the corn patch." He wouldn't add that he had wasted an arrow and watched the porcupine waddle off unharmed.

Perhaps, after all, those lessons hadn't been entirely wasted.

⮑ CHAPTER 14 ⮐

ROBINSON CRUSOE HAD COME TO AN END. MATT HAD skipped more than half of it, choosing only the pages where there was plenty of action. Now he was sorry it had not lasted longer. Attean also seemed disappointed.

"Too bad," he commented, copying one of Matt's frequent remarks. "I tell story to brothers. Every night I tell more story. They like."

Delighted, Matt tried to picture the Indians sitting around the campfire at night listening to Attean tell the story of Robinson Crusoe. He would give a good deal to hear Attean's version of it. Now suddenly he had an inspiration.

"If they want more stories, I have lots of them," he exclaimed.

He took his father's Bible from the shelf. Why hadn't he thought of this before? Why, there was Samson! David and Goliath! Joseph and his coat of many colors!

"They're even better than *Robinson Crusoe*," he promised.

It really was true. The ancient Bible stories were filled with adventure. And they were told straight out in simple language that didn't need skipping.

He began with the story of Noah. How God warned Noah that a great flood was coming. How Noah built the ark and took inside his family and two of every kind of animal. How they all lived in the ark safely while it rained for forty days and forty nights. How Noah sent a dove out three times, and when it came back the third time with a twig of olive in its beak, Noah knew that the flood was over. Here Matt looked up to see a grin on Attean's face.

"Beaver people tell story like that," he said. "Very old story. You want me tell?"

Matt waited curiously.

"Very long time," Attean began, scowling as he tried to translate from his own tongue, "before animal, was great rain. Water came over all the land. One Indian go to very high hill, climb very high tree. Rain many days. Water come up to feet of Indian, but no more. Gluskabe bring three ducks to Indian. One day he let one duck go. It fly away and not come back. Other day he let other duck go. It not come back. Then last duck come back with mud in mouth. Indian know water go down. When water all gone, he come down from tree. He make grass. Make bird and animal. Make man and beaver. Man and beaver make all other Indians.

"Golly," said Matt. "It's almost like the Bible story. Where did the Indians get it?"

Attean shrugged. "Very old story. Indians take long time to tell. I not know white man's words."

"You told it fine. But who was this Glu — whatever you called him?"

"Gluskabe. Mighty hunter. Come from north. Very strong. He make wind blow. Make thunder. He make all animal. Make Indian."

Matt was puzzled. He had heard that the Indians worshipped the Great Spirit. This Gluskabe did not sound like a Great Spirit. He sounded more like one of the heroes in the old folk tales his mother had told him when he was a child. He decided it would be impolite to ask more. He wondered if the Indians had many stories like that. And how could it be that here in the forest they had learned about the flood?

~CHAPTER 15~

ON THE DAY OF THEIR GREATEST ADVENTURE, Attean had come without his dog. So there was no warning.

Matt was in fine spirits that day, because he had managed by a magnificent stroke of luck to hit a rabbit with his bow and arrow. It was the first time this had happened, and it was more the rabbit's doing than his own. The silly creature had just sat there and let him take careful aim. All the same, he was pleased with himself, and even more pleased that Attean had been there to see it.

When the boys decided to visit the beaver dam again, Matt was unwilling to leave the rabbit behind in case some thieving animal should discover it. He was walking behind Attean, swinging the rabbit carelessly by the ears as Attean always did, when the Indian suddenly halted, his whole body tensed. Matt could see nothing unusual, and he had opened his mouth to speak, when Attean silenced him with a jerk of his hand. Then he heard a sound in the underbrush ahead. Not a rustle like a grouse or a snake. Not a trapped animal. This was a stirring of something moving slowly and heavily.

He felt a cold prickle in his stomach. He stood beside Attean, his own muscles tight, scarcely breathing.

A low bush bent sideways. Through the leaves a brown head thrust itself. Bigger than that of a dog, and shaggier. It was a small bear cub. Matt could see the little eyes peering at them curiously, the brown nose wrinkling at the strange smell of human boy. The little animal looked so comical that Matt almost laughed out loud.

"Hsst!" Attean warned under his breath.

There was a crashing of bush and a low, snarling growl. An immense paw reached through the thicket and tumbled the cub over and out of sight. In its place loomed a huge brown shape. Bursting through the leaves was a head three times as big as the cub's. No curiosity in those small eyes, only an angry reddish gleam.

Somehow Matt had the sense not to run. He stood frozen on the path. A bear could overtake a running man in a few bounds. And this one was only two bounds away. The bear's head moved slowly from side to side. Its heavy body brushed aside the branches as though they were cobwebs. It swayed, shifting its weight from one foot to the other. Slowly it rose on its hind legs. Matt could see the wicked curving claws.

Matt would never know why he acted as he did. He could not remember thinking at all, only staring with numb horror at the creature about to charge. Somehow he did move. He swung the dead rabbit by its ears and hurled it straight at the bear's head. The tiny body struck the bear squarely on its nose. With a jerk of her head the bear shook it off as though it were a buzzing mosquito. The rabbit flopped useless to the ground. The bear did not even bother to look down at it. She had been distracted for only an instant, but in that instant something flashed through the air. There was a sharp twang and the dull thud of a blow. Just between the eyes of the bear, the shaft of Attean's arrow quivered. As the waving forepaws began to lower, a second arrow struck just below the bear's shoulder.

The great head shuddered and sank toward the ground. With a wild yell, Attean sprang forward and thrust his knife deep, just behind his first arrow. Still scarcely aware that he moved at all, Matt leaped after him. Jerking his own knife from his belt, he sank it into brown fur. His blow had been misplaced, but it was not needed. The bear's sides were heaving. The boys stood watching, and in a few moments it lay still.

Matt stared down at the creature in horror. The fearsome yellow teeth were still bared in a snarl. Saliva and blood dribbled down from the open jaws. The little eyes that had glittered so savagely were filmed over. The long, sharp claws hung powerless, clotted with pawed-up earth.

Now that there was nothing to fear, Matt felt his knees shaking. He hoped that Attean would not notice, and he managed a wide grin to hide his trembling. But Attean did not grin back. He stood over the bear, and he began to speak, slowly and solemnly, in his own tongue. He spoke for some time.

"What were you saying?" Matt demanded when the speaking was over.

"I tell bear I do not want to kill," Attean answered. "Indian not kill she-bear with cub. I tell bear we did not come here to hunt."

"But it might have killed us both!"

"Maybe. I ask bear to forgive that I must kill."

"Well, I'm mighty thankful you did," Matt said stoutly. He was about to say that he had never been so scared in his life, but he thought better of it.

Attean looked at him, and his solemnness suddenly dissolved in a grin. "You move quick," he said. "Like Indian."

Matt felt his cheeks turn red. "You killed him," he said honestly. Yet he knew that he had had a part. He had given Attean just that instant in which to notch his arrow.

Attean nudged the bear with his toe. "Small," he said. "Just same fat. Good for eat."

Small! That monstrous creature! It certainly was too big for two boys to carry. It appeared that Attean had no intention of trying.

"Belong squaw now," he said. "I go tell."

"You mean a squaw is going to carry that heavy thing?"

"Cut up meat, then carry. Squaw work," Attean answered. It was plain that he had done the man's work and was finished with it.

"The cub," Matt remembered now. It was nowhere in sight.

Attean shook his head. "Let cub go," he said. "When *sigwan* come again, him plenty big to eat.

"Take rabbit," Attean reminded him.

Matt looked with distaste at the rabbit, almost covered by the bear's heavy paw, the fur matted and bloody. He would rather not have touched it, but obediently he pulled it out. It was his dinner, after all. And he knew that in Attean's world everything that was killed must be used. The Indians did not kill for sport.

When Attean had disappeared into the forest, Matt still stood looking down at the first bear he had ever seen. He felt resentful. Attean had killed the bear, of course. It was his by right. But Matt would have liked just a small share of that meat, or even one of those big claws to show his father. Then he remembered the Indian boy's tribute. He had moved fast, like an Indian. That would have to be share enough.

CHAPTER 16

IN THE LATE AFTERNOON MATT SAT IN THE CABIN doorway. He couldn't think of any work to do. He felt restless, the excitement still jumping about inside him. He needed to talk to someone. He wanted to tell his father about the bear. Thinking of his father, he felt that snake of worry crawling about behind every other thought. That worry was becoming more frequent every day. What could have kept his father so long?

Suppose some accident had befallen him? The meeting with the bear had shaken Matt's trust in the forest. Now it seemed to close him in on every side, dark and threatening. Suppose his father had met with a bear? Suppose he had never got back to Quincy? How would his mother know where to find this place, or even where to send anyone to look for him? Matt hugged his arms around his chest. But the cold was inside. It would not go away.

Something moved at the edge of the woods. Matt leaped to his feet. A stranger came walking into the clearing. With an ugly chill against his backbone, Matt stared at the hideously painted face. Then he recognized Attean, a very different Attean from the boy who had walked with him in the forest that morning.

The Indian boy had washed his body, and it shone with fresh grease. He had combed his tangled black locks. Down his cheeks on either side and on his forehead ran broad streaks of blue and white paint. On a cord around his neck dangled a row of new bear's claws.

In case Attean had noticed his first alarm, Matt greeted him boldly. "What's the war paint for?" he demanded.

"Not war paint," Attean answered. "Squaws make feast with bear. My grandfather say you come."

Matt hesitated, unable to believe his ears. It took him a moment to realize that this was actually an invitation.

"Thanks," he stammered. "I'd sure like some of that bear meat. Wait till I get my jacket."

"Shut door," Attean reminded him. "Maybe another bear come." Attean was in a good humor. He had made one of his unexpected jokes.

"Long way," Attean said, after a time. Matt was certain they must have been walking fast for more than an hour. He remembered that Attean had already walked all this way to fetch him and he kept silent. It was so dark now that he could barely see to put one foot before the other, but he realized that they were on a well-beaten trail. Just as the last light was glinting above the treetops, they reached a river bank. Drawn up at its edge was a small birch canoe. Attean motioned him to step into it. Then he gave a push and leaped nimbly into the stern. His paddle moved soundlessly. Grateful to sit still, Matt was entranced by the speed, the silence, the gliding shadows on the silver river. He was regretful when in a very few strokes they reached the other side.

Now Matt could see a glimmer of light deep in the woods. Attean led him toward it, and presently their way was barred by a solid wall of upright posts. A stockade. For the first time a quiver of uneasiness made Matt falter. But stronger than any doubt, curiosity drove him on. Not for one moment would he have turned back. Eagerly he followed Attean through a gateway into an open space filled with smoke and moving shadows and wavering patches of light cast by birchbark torches.

All around him in a circle rose the dim shapes of cabins and cone-shaped wigwams. In the center of the circle a long, narrow fire was burning between walls of logs. Suspended on timbers hung three iron pots, sending up rosy curls of steam in the smoky air. The fragrance of boiling meat and pungent herbs made Matt's stomach crawl.

Then he was aware of the Indians. They sat silently on either side of the fire, their painted faces ghastly in the flickering light. They were clad in an odd medley of garments, some in Englishmen's coats and jackets, others with bright blankets draping their shoulders. A few had feathers standing straight up from headbands. Everywhere there was the gleam of metal on arms and chests. Women in bright cloth skirts and odd pointed caps moved about without a sound, adding wood to the fire or stirring the contents of the kettles. Light glinted on their silver armbands and necklaces. Clearly the Indians had put on their finest array for this feast. It came over Matt with a rush of shame how very shabby he must look in their eyes. Even if Attean had warned

78

him, what could he have done? He had no other clothes to wear. Probably Attean had known that and so had said nothing.

No one seemed to notice him. Yet he was conscious of the unblinking stare of the row facing him. The others did not turn their heads. They seemed to be waiting. In the silence, Matt's heart beat so loudly they all surely must have heard it.

After a long pause, one man rose slowly and came toward him. It was Saknis, his paint-streaked face barely recognizable. He wore a long red coat decorated by a handsome beaded collar and metal armbands. A crown of feathers rose from the beaded band around his forehead. He stood very tall, and there was pride in his stern features. Why, Matt thought, he looked like a king!

"*Kweh*," Saknis said with dignity. "White boy welcome."

In a sudden terrifying yell the rows of Indians echoed this greeting. "*Ta ho*," they shouted. "*Ta ho. Ye hye hye.*"

"*Kweh*," Matt stammered in return, then more boldly, "*Kweh.*"

The Indians seemed satisfied. Smiles flashed in their dark faces. There was rough laughter, and then, seeming to forget him, they began to jabber to each other. From nowhere, children suddenly crowded around him, giggling, daring each other to touch him. Matt's heart slowed its pounding. There was nothing to fear in this place, but after the weeks of stillness in his cabin the noise was confusing. He was grateful when Attean came to his rescue and led him to a seat at the end of a log. An old woman approached and held out to him a gourd cup. It contained a sweetish drink, acid and flavored with maple sugar, good on his dry tongue.

Saknis raised his arm, and instantly the clamor was silenced. There was no doubt Attean's grandfather was the leader here. An Indian brought him a long pipe and Saknis put it to his lips and slowly blew out a long wreath of smoke. The rows of Indians waited respectfully for him to speak. Instead the old man turned to his grandson and held out the pipe.

Attean stepped into the center of the clearing. In the firelight he stood straight and slender, his bare arms and legs gleaming. Matt had never seen him like this. Proudly he took the pipe, set it briefly to his own lips, and handed it back to his grandfather. Then he began to speak.

Matt did not need to understand the words. He soon realized that Attean was recounting the morning's adventure. Watching his gestures, Matt felt himself living again the walk through the woods, the meeting with the small cub, the fearsome mother about to charge. As Attean spoke, the Indians urged the boy on with grunts and shouts of approval and pleasure. Attean tensed his body. He uttered a sharp cry, pointed at Matt, and made a flinging sweep of his arm, hurling an imaginary rabbit. The seated figures broke into loud cries, shouting "*He*," grinning and pointing at Matt, swinging their own arms in imitation. Matt's cheeks were hot. He knew they were making fun of him. But boisterous as it was, the sound was friendly. Now they turned back to Attean and followed his story with growing excitement.

Attean certainly made a very good story of it. His telling took a lot longer than the actual event. Plainly they all enjoyed it, and in listening they were all taking part in it. Attean was a skillful storyteller. Matt could understand now just how he must have delighted them with his acting out of *Robinson Crusoe*.

When the narrative was over, the Indians sprang to their feet. They formed a long line. Then began a sound that sent a tingle, half dread and half pleasure, down Matt's spine. A lone Indian had leaped to the head of the line, beating a rattle against his palm in an odd, stirring rhythm. He strutted and pranced in ridiculous contortions, for all the world like a clown in a village fair. The line of figures followed after him, aping him and stamping their feet in response.

Attean was at his side again. "Dance now," he said. "Then feast."

The rhythm of the rattle quickened. The line of figures wove round the fire, faster and faster. Women joined now, at the end of the line, linking their arms, swaying. Finally the children, even small children, were dancing, stamping their small naked feet.

"Dance," Attean commanded. He seized Matt's arm and pulled him into the moving line. The men near him cheered him on, laughing at Matt's stumbling attempts. Once he caught his breath, Matt found it simple to follow the step. His confidence swelled as the rhythm throbbed through his body, loosening his tight muscles. He was suddenly filled with excitement and happiness. His own heels pounded against the hard ground. He was one of them.

He came back to earth with a stitch in his side. His legs threatened to give way under him. The dancing seemed to have no end. Determined that Attean should not see him weakening, he moved faster and stamped harder. Finally, when he felt he could not make the circle one more time, the dance ended.

The feasting began. A squaw brought him a wooden bowl filled with thick, hot stew and a curiously carved wooden spoon. The first steaming mouthful burned his tongue, but he was too hungry to wait. He thought nothing had ever tasted so good, dark and greasy and spicy. So this was bear meat!

Presently he noticed that Attean sat beside him, eating nothing.

"You're not eating," he said, with a sudden doubt. "Have you given me your share?"

"This my bear," the boy answered. "I kill. Not eat. Maybe not get any more bear." He didn't sound as if he minded in the least, as if, in fact, he was proud of not eating.

When Matt's bowl was empty, the squaw refilled it. By the time he finished, sleepiness began to drag at his eyelids. He could scarcely hold them open. Attean seemed in no hurry to leave. The Indians were enjoying themselves, refilling their bowls, shouting at each other, laughing and slapping their legs at what seemed to be uproarious jokes. This was noisier than any celebration Matt had ever seen in Quincy, even on Muster Day. Why had he ever had the idea that the Indians were a dull lot?

At last, however, they fell silent, and Matt saw that one of them was beginning another story. It promised to be a long one. Between the sentences the speaker drew on his pipe, and the smoke curled from his nose and mouth as he spoke. Matt's head drooped and came up with a painful jerk. He had almost fallen asleep sitting up. Attean laughed and motioned him to his feet. At the thought of tramping all the way back to the cabin, Matt groaned. It must be close to midnight.

Then he saw that Attean did not mean to go back. He led Matt toward one of the wigwams and pulled back the flap of deerskin that hung across the door. Inside, a small fire burned, and by its faint light Matt saw a low platform covered with matting and fur. Attean made a silent motion, and Matt, too sleepy to question, gratefully let his tired body sink down on the soft skins. Attean stirred up the fire and left him alone. Once, long after, Matt roused to hear the rattle and the pounding of feet. The Indians were dancing again, and he was thankful to stay right where he was.

CHAPTER 17

WHEN MATT WOKE, THE WIGWAM WAS DIM, BUT the cracks of brightness around the doorflap showed that it was daylight. By the sounds, the village was up and about. He could hear men's voices, the shouts of children, and the shrill yelping of dogs. Behind these sounds there beat a dull thumping rhythm. Could the Indians still be dancing?

He lay looking about him, at the smoke-streaked walls of woven matting, at the clutter of objects hanging here and there — shapeless garments, cooking pots, odd-shaped bags of animal skin, bundles of dried grasses and herbs. Under the platform where he had slept was an untidy pile of baskets and rolled-up mats. From the heap of ashes in the center of the dirt floor a wisp of smoke curled upward toward the small hole in the roof. Much of it could not escape and drifted back to hang in thin clouds just above his head. Matt's throat felt tight with it, and he sat up, coughing. Then he moved to the doorway, pushed back the flap, and stepped outside.

As though they had been waiting, children came scuffling about him, their bright eyes curious. Most of them were naked as little frogs.

"*Kweh,*" he said uncertainly, sending them into a chorus of giggles. Matt was relieved to see Attean approaching.

"You sleep long time," Attean greeted him. "Too much bear, reckon."

Matt smiled shamefacedly. He still found it hard to take Attean's sober teasing.

Over the heads of the children he looked about the village. Last night, in the darkness and firelight, it had appeared mysterious and awesome. Now, under the strong sunlight, he saw that it was shabby and cluttered. There were a few bark cabins; for the most part the wigwams were ramshackle and flimsy. On every side, from racks of untrimmed branches, hung rows of drying fish. Scattered heaps of clamshells and animal bones littered the ground. The Indians themselves had discarded the splendor of the night before. Some of them, like Attean, wore only a breechcloth; others, faded cloth trousers and ragged blankets. The women had replaced their bright finery with skirts and vests of dingy blue cotton.

Now he could see what was making that rhythmic thumping. Two women were pounding corn in a huge mortar made from a tree trunk, their arms alternately rising and falling. Others nearby were grinding in smaller mortars of hollowed stones. They sat close together, jabbering like bluejays, but their chatter did not for an instant interfere with the steady rhythm of their bare arms. In front of another wigwam, two women were weaving baskets of rushes. As Matt and

Attean passed them, they looked up with shy smiles. All the women, Matt noticed, were hard at work. A few very old men sat smoking in front of the wigwams, and a group of boys squatted in a circle playing at some sort of game.

"Where are the men?" he asked.

"Gone," Attean said. "Before sun up. My grandfather lead hunt for deer."

He had brought a hunk of corn bread for each of them, and munching it they walked through the village back to the canoe. Matt kept hanging back, looking all about him at the village. He wanted to stay longer. There were a hundred questions he longed to ask. But Attean seemed impatient; his genial mood of the night before had vanished. Without wasting a motion, he pushed the canoe into the water. A taggle of children had followed them and now stood on the bank, laughing and waving as they moved out into the river.

Matt tried to find a reason for Attean's silence. "If it hadn't been for me," he asked, "would you have gone on the deer hunt with the men?"

Attean did not like the question. "Not take me," he admitted finally. "I not have gun."

"You're a good shot with a bow and arrow."

Attean scowled. "That old way," he said. "Good for children. Indian hunt now with white man's gun. Someday my grandfather buy me gun. Need many beaver skins. Beaver not so many now."

"I know guns cost a lot," Matt said. "I'll have to wait a good while for another one myself." Attean had long since heard the story of Ben's visit.

"White man can buy with money," Attean said. "Indian not have money. One time plenty wampum. Now wampum no good to pay for gun."

There was bitterness in Attean's voice. Matt understood now why Attean had defended the beaver dam so fiercely. Was it true that beaver were getting scarce? Matt thought of the village they had just left, how very poor it seemed, how few possessions the Indians could boast. For the first time Matt glimpsed how it might be for them, watching their old hunting grounds taken over by white settlers and by white traders demanding more skins than the woods could provide. As they set off through the forest he tried to think of a way to lift Attean's gloom.

"That was a mighty fine feast," he said. "And I was glad to see where you live. I'd like to go there again someday."

Attean's scowl only deepened. "My grandmother not want you come to feast," he said finally. "My grandfather say you must. She say you not sleep in her house."

"Oh," said Matt lamely, his own pleasure suddenly dimmed. So many things were suddenly clear to him: why he had been left alone to sleep in the empty wigwam; why Attean had hurried him away so abruptly this morning. Attean had been caught in a family argument and was annoyed about it.

"My grandmother hate all white men," Attean said.

When Matt could find nothing to answer, Attean went on. "White man kill my mother. She go out with two squaw to find bark for make basket. White man come through woods and shoot with gun. My mother

87

do them no harm. We no longer at war with white men. Just same they kill for get scalp. White men get money for Indian scalp. Even scalp of children."

Matt's indignant protest never got past his throat. He remembered that it was true, or had been a long time ago. He had heard that during the war the Massachusetts governor had offered a bounty for Indian scalps. Attean must have been a very small child.

"My father go out on war trail," Attean said. "He go to find white man who killed my mother. He not come back."

Matt was speechless. He had never dreamed that anything like this lay behind Attean's carefree life. He had never wondered about Attean's parents at all, only accepted without question that the boy followed his grandfather and obeyed him.

"No wonder she hates us," he said at last. "Terrible things always happen when there's a war — on both sides. You've got to admit, Attean, that there was a reason. The Indians did the same thing to white settlers. The white women were afraid to go outside their cabins."

"Why white men make cabins on Indian hunting grounds?"

Matt had no answer to that. It was no use, he thought. The war with the French was over. The Indians and the English had made peace. But the hatred — would that ever be over? For all he and Attean walked through the woods together, there was a wall between them that Attean would never forget. In sudden panic he thought of his own mother. Was it right for his father to bring her to this place?

"Does your grandfather hate us too?" he asked.

Attean did not answer at first. Finally he said, "My grandfather say Indian must learn to live with white man."

It was not the answer Matt had hoped for. But Saknis had said he must come to the feast. In spite of the grandmother, Saknis had made him welcome.

"When my father comes," he said, "I want him to know your grandfather. I think they would like each other."

Attean did not answer, and they walked on in silence. Discomforted, Matt turned his attention to the trail they were following. Presently he recognized the unmistakable carving of a little animal cut into the bark of a tree. But when he turned to Attean to boast of his recognition, he was silenced by the darkness in Attean's eyes. Instead, without speaking, he studied the signs they passed. He marked fallen trees pointing along the path, small piles of stones, and, wherever the trail seemed to vanish, he discovered on a tree the sign of the beaver. When they came out at last on a trail he knew well, he marked carefully the spot where the two trails met. Why, he thought in sudden excitement, I could actually find my way to that village. I'm sure I could. But he did not share his thought with Attean. He knew that unless Attean took him there he could never go to that village again. Saknis had only invited him to the feast out of kindness, or perhaps out of fairness for his small share in killing the bear. Would he ever be given another chance?

CHAPTER 18

OVER AND OVER, THOUGH HE KNEW THE NUMBER only too well, Matt counted his notched sticks. He kept hoping he had made a mistake. Always they were the same. Ten sticks. That meant that August had long since gone by. He couldn't remember exactly how many days belonged to each month, but any way he reckoned it the month of September must be almost over. He only needed to look about him. The maple trees circling the clearing flamed scarlet. The birches and aspens glowed yellow, holding a sunlight of their own even on misty days. The woods had become quieter. Jays still screamed at him, and chickadees twittered softly in the trees, but the songbirds had disappeared. Twice he had heard a faraway trumpeting and had seen long straggles of wild geese like trailing smoke high in the air, moving south. In the morning, when he stepped out of the cabin, the frosty air nipped his nose. The noonday was warm as midsummer, but when he came inside at dusk he hurried to stir up the fire. There was a chilliness inside him as well that neither the sun nor the fire ever quite reached. It seemed to him that day by day the shadow of the forest moved closer to the cabin.

Why was his family so late in coming?

He was troubled too because the autumn weather seemed to have brought about a restlessness in Attean. There were days when the Indian boy did not come. He never offered a word of explanation. After a day or two he would simply walk into the cabin and sit down at the table. He rarely suggested that they hunt or fish together. Day after day Matt tramped the woods alone, trying to shake the doubts that walked beside him like his own shadow.

As he walked, Matt was careful to cut blazes in the bark of trees. They gave him courage to walk farther into the forest than he had ever dared before, since he was sure of finding his way back to the cabin. He also watched for Indian signs, and sometimes he was sure he had detected one. One day, looking up, he saw on a nearby tree the sign of the turtle. Time to turn back, he told himself. He felt secure now in the territory of the beaver, but he wasn't so certain that a strange people would welcome a white trespasser.

As he started to retrace his steps, he heard, some distance away, the sharp, high-pitched yelp of a dog. It didn't sound threatening, but neither did it sound like the happy, excited bark of a hound that had scented a rabbit. It sounded almost like the scream of a child. When it came again, it died away into a low whining, and he remembered the trapped fox.

Attean had warned him to have nothing to do with a turtle trap. But he hesitated, and the sound came again. No matter what Attean had told him, he could not bring himself to walk away from that sound. Warily, he made his way through the brush.

It was a dog, a scrawny Indian dog, dirt-caked and bloody. As Matt moved closer he saw, through the blood, the white streak down the side of its face, then the chewed ear and the stubby porcupine quills. Only one dog in the world looked like that. It was caught by its foreleg, just as the fox had been, and it was frantic with pain and fear. Its eyes were glazed, and white foam dripped from its open jaws. Matt felt his own muscles tense with anger. His mind was made up in an instant. It had been bad enough to leave a fox to suffer. Turtle tribe or no, he was not going to walk away from Attean's dog. Somehow he had to get that dog out of the trap.

But how? As he bent down, the dog snapped at him so ferociously that he jumped back. Even if it recognized him, Attean's dog had never learned to trust him. Now it was too crazed to understand that Matt meant to help. Matt set his teeth and stooped again. This time he got his hands on the steel bands of the trap and gave a tug. With a deep growl, the dog snapped at him again. Matt started, scraping his hand against the steel teeth. He leaped to his feet and stared at the red gash that ran from his knuckles to his wrist. It was no use, he realized. There was no way he could get that trap open with the dog in this maddened state. Somehow he would have to find Attean.

He began to run through the forest, back over the way he had come, back along the trails he knew, searching his memory for the signs he remembered that led to the Indian village. Luck was with him. There was the sign of the beaver cut into a tree, and here were the fallen logs. He was never absolutely sure, but he knew he walked in the right direction, and after nearly an hour, to his great relief, he came out on the shore of the river. There was no canoe waiting, as there had been when Attean had led him there. But the river was narrow, and placid. Thank goodness he had grown up near the ocean, and his father had taken him swimming from the time he could walk. He left his moccasins hidden under a bush and plunged in. In a few moments he came out, dripping, within sight of the stockade.

He was greeted by a frenzied barking of dogs. They burst through the stockade and rushed toward him, halting only a few feet away, menacing him so furiously that he dared not take another step. Behind them came a group of girls who quieted the dogs with shrill cries and blows.

"I have come for Attean," Matt said, when he could make himself heard.

The girls stared at him. Tired, wet, and ashamed of showing his fear of the dogs, Matt could not summon up any politeness or dignity. "Attean," he repeated impatiently.

One girl, bolder than the others, answered him, flaunting her knowledge of the white man's language. "Attean not here," she told him.

"Then Saknis."

"Saknis not here. All gone hunt."

Desperately Matt seized his only remaining chance. "Attean's grandmother," he demanded. "I must see her."

The girls looked at each other uneasily. Matt pulled

back his shoulders and tried to put into his voice the stern authority that belonged to Saknis. "It is important," he said. "Please show me where to find her."

Amazingly, his blustering had an effect. After some whispering, the girls moved back out of his way.

"Come," the leading girl ordered, and he followed her through the gate.

He was not surprised that she led him straight to the most substantial cabin in the clearing. He had recognized on the night of the feast that Saknis was a chief. Now facing him in the doorway was a figure even more impressive than the old man. She was an aging woman, gaunt and wrinkled, but still handsome. Her black braids were edged with white. She stood erect, her lips set in a forbidding line, her eyes brilliant, with no hint of welcome. Could he make her understand? Matt wondered in confusion.

"I'm sorry, ma'am," he began. "I know you don't want me to come here. I need help. Attean's dog is caught in a trap, a steel trap. I tried to open it, but the dog won't let me near it."

The woman stared at him. He could not tell whether she had understood a word. He started to speak again, when the deerskin curtain was pushed aside and a second figure stood in the doorway. It was a girl, with long black braids hanging over her shoulders. She was dressed in blue, with broad bands of red and white beading. Strange, Matt thought, how much alike they looked, the old woman and the girl, standing side by side so straight and proud.

"Me Marie, sister of Attean," the girl said in a soft,

low voice. "Grandmother not understand. I tell what you say."

Matt repeated what he had said and then waited impatiently while she spoke to her grandmother. The woman listened. Finally her grim lips parted in a single scornful phrase.

"*Aremus piz wat*," she said. Good-for-nothing dog.

Matt's awe vanished in anger. "Tell her maybe it is good for nothing," he ordered the girl. "Attean is fond of it. And it's hurt, hurt bad. We've got to get it out of that trap."

There was distress in the girl's eyes as she turned again to her grandmother. He could see that she was pleading, and that in spite of herself the old woman was relenting. After a few short words, the girl went into the cabin and came back in a moment holding in her hand a large chunk of meat, a small blanket folded over her arm.

"Me go with you," she said. "Dog know me."

In his relief, Matt forgot the torn hand he had been holding behind him. Instantly the old woman moved forward and snatched at it. Her eyes questioned him.

"It's nothing," he said hastily. "I almost got the trap open."

She gave his arm a tug, commanding him to follow her.

"There isn't time," he protested.

She silenced him with a string of words of which he understood only the scornful *piz wat*.

"She say dog not go away," the girl explained. "Better you come. Trap maybe make poison."

Having no choice, Matt followed them into the cabin. He saw now that the woman's straight posture had been a matter of pride. She was really very lame, and stooped as she walked ahead of him. While she busied herself over the fire, he sat obediently on a low platform and looked about him. He was astonished that the little room, strange, and so unlike his mother's kitchen, seemed beautiful. It was very clean. The walls were lined with birchbark and hung with woven mats and baskets of intricate design. The air was sweet with fresh grasses spread on the earth floor.

Without speaking, the woman tended him, washing his hand with clean warm water. From a painted gourd she scooped a pungent-smelling paste and spread it over the wound, then bound his hand with a length of clean blue cotton.

"Thank you," Matt said when she had finished. "It feels better."

She dismissed him with a grunting imitation of Saknis's "Good." The girl, who had been watching, moved swiftly to the door. As Matt rose to follow her, the grandmother held out to him a slab of corn bread. He had not realized how hungry he was, and he accepted it gratefully.

The girl took the lead, brushing aside the curious children and the still-suspicious dogs. At the river's edge she untied a small canoe, and Matt stepped into it, thankful that his half-dried clothes would not have to be drenched again. Once on the forest trail, she set the pace, and he did not find it easy to keep up with her swift, silent stride. She was so like Attean, though lighter and more graceful.

After a time, Matt ventured to break the silence. "You speak good English," he said.

"Attean tell me about you," she answered. "You tell him good story."

"Attean didn't tell me he had a sister."

The girl laughed. "Attean think squaw girl not good for much," she said. "Attean only like to hunt."

"I have a sister too," he told her. "She's coming soon."

"What she name?"

"Sarah. She's younger than you. But Marie isn't an Indian name, is it?" Matt asked.

"Is Christian name. Me baptized by father."

Attean had never mentioned a priest either, but Matt knew that the French Jesuits had lived with the Indians here in Maine long before the English settlers came.

"When my sister comes, will you come with Attean to see her?" he asked.

"It might be so," she answered politely. She sounded as though it never would be.

At last they heard the yelping just ahead of them and they both began to run. Even in his terror, the dog recognized the girl, and greeted her with a frantic beating of his tail. He gulped at the meat she held out to him. But he still would not let either of them touch the trap. The girl had come prepared for this, and she unfolded the blanket she had carried, threw it over the dog's head, and gathered the folds behind him. With surprising strength, she held the struggling bundle tightly in her arms while Matt took the trap in both hands and slowly forced the jaws open. In a moment the dog was free, escaping the blanket, bounding away from them on three legs, the fourth paw dangling at an odd angle.

"I'm afraid it's broken," Matt said. He was still breathing hard from that last run and from the effort of tugging those steel jaws apart.

"Attean mend," the girl said, folding up the blanket as calmly as though she were simply tidying up a cabin.

The dog hobbled slowly after them along the trail, lying down now and then to lick at the bleeding paw. They made slow progress, and now that the worry was over Matt was aware how tired he was. It seemed as though he had been walking back and forth over that trail all day, and the way to the village seemed endless. He was thankful when, halfway to the river, he saw Attean approaching swiftly along the trail.

"My grandmother send me," he explained. "You get dog out?"

"I couldn't do it alone," Matt admitted.

Attean stood watching as the dog came limping toward him. "Dog very stupid," he said. "No good for hunt. No good for smell turtle smell. What for I take back such foolish dog?"

His harsh words did not fool Matt for a moment. Nor did they fool the dog. The scruffy tail thumped joyfully against the earth. The brown eyes looked up at the Indian boy with adoration. Attean reached into his pouch and brought out a strip of dried meat. Then he bent and very gently took the broken paw into his hands.

&CHAPTER 19&

"GRANDMOTHER SAY YOU COME TO VILLAGE TODAY," Attean announced two days later.

"That's kind of her," Matt answered. "But my hand is just about healed. It doesn't need any more medicine."

"Not for medicine."

Matt waited uncertainly.

"My grandmother very surprise white boy go long way for Indian dog," Attean explained. "She say you welcome."

So once again Matt crossed the river into the Indian stockade. This time, though the dogs barked at him and children stared and giggled, he did not feel so much like a stranger. Saknis held out a hand of welcome. Attean's grandmother did not exactly smile, but her thin lips were less grim. Behind her, Attean's sister smiled but did not speak. The old woman dipped a clamshell ladle into a kettle and filled three bowls with a stew of fish and corn, then drew back while Attean and Saknis and Matt ate their meal in silence. Neither she nor Marie ate till the men were finished.

After the meal Attean did not hurry him away. He rather grandly played host and led Matt about the village. He was amused when Matt kept stopping every few feet to watch what the women were doing. Matt was filled with curiosity. He knew well enough that Attean was scornful of the squaw work the white boy had to do, but Attean didn't have to worry about what he was going to eat next day. There were so many things Matt wanted to learn. He observed carefully as two women pounded dried kernels of corn between two rounded stones, catching the coarse flour on a strip of birchbark. He marked how they spread berries on bark, so that the sun dried them hard as pebbles. He admired the baskets made of a single strip of birchbark, bent and fastened at the corners so tightly that water could be boiled inside. "I must remember that," he resolved. "I could do that myself if I tried."

For a time Attean good-naturedly answered his questions; finally he grew impatient of squaw work. He led Matt toward a cluster of boys who squatted in a circle in the dirt pathway, absorbed in some noisy game. The boys widened their ring to make room for two more, and Matt crouched awkwardly on his heels to watch them.

One after the other, they were shaking six smooth bone discs in a wooden bowl and tossing them out onto the ground. Each disc was marked on one side with a band of red paint. When each boy had had a turn, the one who had thrown the most discs to land painted-side up was proclaimed the winner, and with much gloating he collected from each of the others a number of small sticks. Then they handed the bowl to Matt. His luck was good. Five of the discs showed red bands, and with laughter and clowning the others piled up before him a little heap of sticks.

What was so exciting about this simple game, he wondered, to cause so much shouting? The bowl went rapidly round the circle, the sticks kept changing hands, and presently he had the answer. One of the boys had no sticks left to pay. With a mocking groan he unclasped from his arm a wide copper band and tossed it to the winner.

So that's it, Matt thought silently. Sooner or later I'm bound to lose too, and when I do, what will they expect me to forfeit?

He did not have long to wait. At his next turn every one of the discs landed blank side up. Ruefully he handed over the last of the sticks he had won. There was a gleeful shout, and then they waited.

What do I have? he thought desperately. Nothing in his pocket but his jackknife, and his very life depended upon that knife.

Then the boy nearest him reached over and jerked roughly at the sleeve of his shirt. Matt pretended not to understand, and the boy tugged harder. Two of the others got to their feet, plainly ready to tear the shirt from his back. Attean made no move to help him. Grimly he pulled the shirt over his head and tossed it to the winner. It served him right, he supposed. His father had always forbidden him to gamble. But what was he going to do without that shirt? It was the only one he had.

Now Attean put an end to the game. He leaped to

his feet and produced from nowhere a soft ball made of deerskin. Instantly the others raced off in all directions and came back carrying thin sticks. One of these was thrust at Matt. It was a curious sort of bat, light and flexible, with a wide, flat curve at the tip. Forgetting his humiliation, Matt suddenly grinned. With a bat in his hand he could hold his own with any Indian. The boys back in Quincy could have told them that. Eagerly he joined in the scramble of choosing sides.

But never had he played a game like this, so fast and merciless. The ball could not be touched by hand or foot. It was kept flying through the air by the sticks alone. If it fell to the ground, some player scooped it up with the tip of his bat and sent it spinning again. The Indian boys were bewilderingly quick and skillful, and they wielded their bats with no heed for each other's heads, and certainly not for Matt's. It was no accident, he knew, when an elbow jabbed suddenly into his right eye. These boys were putting him to the test. Ignoring the blows that fell on his head and shoulders, Matt swung grimly at the whirling ball, missing it over and over, but sometimes feeling the satisfying thwack of bat against leather. He was thankful now that he had no shirt. If only he could be wearing a breechcloth instead of tight English breeches! But there was no time for worrying about his clothes. Finally, by pure luck, he sent the ball into the hole in the ground that marked the goal. Out of breath and dripping, he grinned as his side generously cheered him and whacked his sore shoulders.

Then, with a whoop, they raced all together through the stockade gate down to the river and went leaping like frogs into the water. Matt floated face down, grateful for the coolness against his burning cheeks. All at once a brown arm circled his neck and dragged him under. Squirming free, he seized a black head in both hands, and the two boys went down together. They came up gasping and grinning. Suddenly Matt was enjoying himself. It was almost as good as being back in Quincy again.

The sun had reached the tops of the pines when he went to Attean's cabin to bid the grandmother goodbye. She stood studying him, and he flushed under her sharp eyes. He must look a sight, he knew. There was a lump as big as an egg on his forehead, and his right eye was probably turning black. She turned and spoke a few stern words to Attean. With a shrug, he went out and returned in a few moments carrying Matt's shirt.

"They play trick on you," he grinned. "Joke."

"Some joke," Matt retorted. He wanted to refuse the shirt, but he couldn't afford to be proud about his only shirt. Resentfully he pulled it over his head.

Before they left, the old woman gave each of them a slab of cake heavy with nuts and berries. Her eyes, as she looked at her grandson, were warm and bright. Matt was minded how his mother had often looked at him, pretending to be angry with him but not able to hide that she was mighty fond of him just the same. Suddenly he felt a sharp stab of homesickness.

Outside the cabin Attean's dog was waiting. He

limped after them to the river, and when Matt stepped into the canoe the dog jumped in after him and settled down only a few inches from Matt's knees. He had never willingly come so close before.

Attean noticed and commented. "Dog remember."

Was that possible? Matt wondered. Could a dog caught in a trap, even though he snapped out in pain and fear, sense that someone was trying to help him? Could the dog remember that terrible ordeal at all? You couldn't read a dog's mind. But just possibly a dog could read a white boy's mind. Very slowly Matt reached down and laid his hand on the dog's back. The dog did not stir or growl. Gently, Matt scratched behind the ragged ear. Gradually, against the bottom of the canoe, the thin tail began to thump in a contented rhythm.

At the opposite bank Attean watched Matt climb out of the canoe, but he did not follow. Apparently this was as far as he intended to go. As Matt hesitated, he lifted his hand. It occurred to Matt that this might be a compliment. Without saying a word, Attean was acknowledging that Matt could now find his own way through the forest. Returning his wave, Matt set out with a confidence he did not quite feel. It was growing dark. He would have to walk fast or he would not be able to mark the signs along the trail.

He was very tired. The bump on his forehead was throbbing. He was sore from head to toe, and his eye was almost swollen shut. But to his surprise, deep inside he felt content. Was it because Attean's dog had finally trusted him? No, more than that had changed.

He had passed some sort of test. Not by any means with flying colors; he had plenty of bruises to remind him of that. But at least he had not disgraced Attean. He felt satisfied. And for the first time since his father had left him, he did not feel alone in the forest.

❦CHAPTER 20❧

FOR THE NEXT FEW DAYS MATT WAITED EAGERLY. Early in the morning he finished his chores, so that at a word from Attean he would be ready to set out for the Indian village again. But Attean did not come. Matt resolved to be patient, but day by day his new confidence began to slide away. Perhaps he had only imagined that he had passed a test. In Attean's eyes perhaps he had failed.

It was a week before Attean came, and the moment Matt saw him he knew that there would be no invitation. The Indian boy was solemn and unsmiling, looking more like his grandfather than ever before. He sat staring at the book Matt opened, his mind plainly miles away. He did not want to listen to a story. He seemed to have forgotten the words he had learned the week before.

"I not remember," he said impatiently. "My grandfather teach me many thing."

"What sort of things?"

Attean did not answer. "Time of hunt come soon," he said finally.

Matt felt suddenly hopeful. Perhaps it was not any failure of his own that had caused Attean to stay away.

Every year, Attean had told him, when the leaves had fallen from the trees, the Indians hunted the caribou and the great moose. Whole families moved away from the village to follow the trail of the big animals. Matt knew that more than anything in the world Attean longed to hunt with the men. He could imagine now how Attean must have been staying close to his grandfather these last days, trying to be useful and to prove that he was fit to be one of them.

"I not come tomorrow," Attean added. "Maybe long time."

"You're going on the hunt!" Matt tried hard to keep the envy out of his voice.

Attean shook his head. "I go to find my manitou."

Matt was puzzled. Was *manitou* another word for moose?

"Maybe you call spirit," Attean explained. "All Indian boy must have manitou. It is time for me."

"How can you find a spirit?" For a moment Matt thought this was one of Attean's odd jokes. But he had never seen his friend so serious. Even troubled.

"My grandfather teach me," Attean repeated. "Manitou come in dream."

Then, seeing that Matt was not laughing, that he really wanted to understand, Attean went on, trying to explain in his clumsy English a mystery that could not truly be explained at all.

Every Indian boy must have a manitou, he said, before he could take his place as one of the men of his family. He had to find it for himself. No one could help him. His grandfather had been training him for many days. He had had to learn many things. Now he must make the test.

He would go out into the forest alone. First, he would make special preparation, bathe himself carefully, and take a special medicine to make him clean inside and out. Then he would go far into the forest and build himself a wigwam of branches. He would stay there alone for many days. He would not eat anything at all, even berries. After sundown he would drink a little water from a brook. He would sing the songs that his grandfather had taught him and repeat the ancient prayers of his people, so that his heart would be worthy. If he did all this, if he waited faithfully, one day his manitou would come to him. Then he could go back to his village. He would have a new name. He would be a man and a hunter.

What would it be like, this manitou? Matt questioned. There was no way to know, Attean told him. It could come in many ways. In a dream he might see a bird or an animal, or even a tree. He might not see anything at all; instead he might hear a voice speaking to him. There would be no mistake. When it came, Attean would recognize that it was meant for him.

"What if the manitou should not come?" Instantly Matt was ashamed of his question. A dark shadow had crossed Attean's face. There was something in his eyes that Matt had never seen there before. Sadness and, more than that, fear.

"I wait," Attean said. "Till he come, I can never be hunter."

Matt could think of nothing at all to say. He felt shut away from his friend in a way that even the boy's scorn had never made him feel. This was something he could not understand or share. If he finds his manitou, he thought, he will go with the men. He may never come here again.

"You'll come back afterwards, won't you?" he asked anxiously, though he knew in his heart that it would never be the same.

"I come back," Attean promised.

Waking in the nights that followed, Matt pulled the blanket tighter about his shoulders. It must be very cold in the forest. He could not get Attean out of his mind. What would it be like, sitting in a shelter, just waiting, growing hungrier every day and more afraid? Because there was no doubt Attean had been afraid, Matt was sure of that. Attean was afraid he might fail, that he might have to return to the village and admit that his manitou had not appeared. For Attean this would be a disgrace, a shame that must be terrible if the thought of it had brought fear into his eyes.

Even though he dreaded that it would mean the end of all their adventures, Matt hoped that Attean would find his manitou.

ᐁᏋCHAPTER 21Ꮶᐅ

THEN ONE MORNING, ATTEAN RETURNED. MATT had been waiting, watching the forest trail impatiently, unwilling to go far from the cabin lest he miss the boy's coming. But when finally he saw Attean approaching, his heart sank. Attean was not alone. His grandfather stalked by his side. Matt sensed that this meant trouble. Perhaps Saknis had come to reproach him. He would surely know that the two boys had been neglecting those lessons. Dreading to face the old man, Matt walked out to meet him, courteously giving the greeting he had learned.

Saknis returned his greeting with dignity. He did not smile. His solemn face made Matt's heart sink still lower. Then, startled, Matt turned toward Attean. He did not dare to ask a question, but he saw at once that there was no need to ask. No doubt about it, Attean had found his manitou. He had changed. He stood straighter and taller. He looked older, and Matt suddenly realized why. The black hair, which had always hung straight down almost to his shoulders, was shaved away. His scalp, like his grandfather's, was bare, except for a single patch running back from his forehead and braided into a topknot fastened with red string. Like the fresh bear grease that glistened on his skin, pride glistened all over him.

Moreover, he carried a gleaming new rifle.

"You've got a gun!" Matt cried, politeness forgotten.

"My grandfather trade many beaver skin," Attean answered. Though he had in these last days become a man, he had not learned altogether to hide his feelings. He did not say more. He waited now for his grandfather to speak.

The old man's face was grave, but he did not ask about the lessons. "Time of sun get shorter," he said, "like footsteps of bird. Soon ice on water."

"I know it's October," Matt said. "Maybe November." He had not wanted to count his sticks these last weeks.

"Indian go north now," Saknis continued. "Hunt moose. All Indians go. Attean not come more to learn white man's signs."

Matt could not answer.

"White father not come," Saknis went on.

Matt spoke quickly. "He ought to be here any day now."

Saknis looked at him soberly. "Maybe him not come," he said quietly.

Anger flared up in Matt. He could not allow this man to speak the fear he had never dared to admit to himself. "Of course he'll come," he said, too loudly. "He might even come today."

"Snow come soon," Saknis persisted. "Not good white boy stay here alone. White boy come with Indians."

Matt stared at him. Did he mean go on the hunt with them? The most important hunt of the year?

Saknis smiled for the first time. "Saknis teach white boy hunt moose like Attean. White boy and Attean be like brother."

A sudden joyful hope sprang into Matt's mind. He realized at this moment just how anxious he had been. This was a way out. He did not have to stay here alone through the long winter. Then, as swiftly as it had come, this new hope died away. In spite of his longing, in spite of being afraid, he knew what he had to answer.

"Thank you," he said. "I'd like to go on the hunt. But I can't do that. If — when my father comes, he wouldn't know where I had gone."

"Leave white man's writing."

Matt swallowed hard. "Something might happen to the cabin. He's trusting me to take care of it."

"Maybe him not come," Saknis said again, not smiling now.

"He'll be here soon," Matt insisted. He was ashamed that his voice broke in the middle of the word. "If he couldn't come, he'd send someone to tell me. He'd find some way, no matter what happened. You don't know my pa."

Saknis was silent for some time. "White boy good son," he said at last. "But better you come. Saknis glad for white boy be *nkweniss*."

Matt could only keep shaking his head. The man's words had brought a great lump in his throat. "Thank you," he managed. "You've been very good to me. But I have to stay here."

Without another word, Saknis held out his hand. Matt put his own hand into that bony grasp. Then the two Indians turned and went away. Attean had not even said goodbye. There would be no lesson that morning. No story. No tramping in the forest, or fishing. Not this morning or any other morning.

Close to panic, Matt wanted to run after them. He wanted to tell them that he had changed his mind. That he would go with them anywhere rather than stay here alone with winter coming on. But he set his jaw tight and stood where he was. After a few minutes he reached for his axe and fell to splitting logs with a fury.

He couldn't keep from thinking, however. Was he just being foolish and stubborn? Wasn't going with them the wisest thing he could have done? Wouldn't his father have understood?

He remembered hearing that many white men — and white women too — who had been captured by the Indians and had lived many years in the wilderness, did not want to return to the white world when they had a chance, but had chosen instead to live with the Indians. He had never understood that, but now he could see very well how it might happen. He no longer distrusted them. He knew that Attean and his grandfather would be kind, that even the grandmother would make him welcome, and that they would share with him whatever they had, no matter how little. He had found friendship and good will in their cabin. He had envied Attean his free, unhampered life in the forest, and the boisterous comradeship in the village. If he had been taken captive as a child and raised as an Indian boy, how would he himself have chosen?

It wouldn't be the same to make that choice deliberately. He was proud that they had wanted him to live with them. But he knew that he could never be really proud, as Attean was proud, of being a hunter. He belonged to his own people. He was bound to his own family, as Attean was bound to his grandfather. The thought that he might never see his mother again was sharper than hunger or loneliness. This was the land his father had cleared to make a home for them all. It was his own land, too. He could not run away.

He was troubled that Attean had walked away without a word of farewell. Had he been offended? Had he really wanted Matt to go with them? To be a brother? Or was he only obeying his grandfather as he had had to do about the lessons? It was so hard to tell what Attean was thinking. Attean had become a hunter. He had a gun. He would not have time now to wander through the forest or to listen to stories. He would not have to bother any longer with a white boy who would never really be a mighty hunter. But surely Attean could have held out his hand, as his grandfather had done.

&CHAPTER 22§

EVERY MORNING, IN SPITE OF HIMSELF, MATT KEPT an eye out for Attean. When four days had gone by he decided there was little chance that he would see his friend again. Doubtless the Indians had already left the village and were on their way north. So when he saw Attean coming through the woods with his dog at his heels he ran across the clearing to meet him, not bothering to hide his relief and pleasure.

"You think different?" Attean asked quickly. "You go with us?"

Matt's eagerness died away. "No," he said unhappily. "Please try to understand, Attean. I must wait for my father."

Attean nodded. "I understand," he said. "My grandfather understand too. I do same for my father if he still live."

The two boys stood looking at each other. There was no amusement and no scorn in Attean's eyes. How very strange, Matt thought. After all the brave deeds he had dreamed of to win this boy's respect, he had gained it at last just by doing nothing, just by staying here and refusing to leave.

"My grandfather send you gift," Attean said now.

He unstrapped from his back a pair of snowshoes. They were new, the wood smooth and polished, the netting of deerhide woven in a neat design. Before Matt could find words, Attean went on.

"My grandmother send gift," he said. He took from his pouch a small birch basket of maple sugar. Late in the season like this, Matt knew, sugar was scarce and dear to the Indians.

"Thank you," he said. "Tell your grandmother that when you come back I'll help gather more sap for her."

Attean was silent. "Not come back," he said then.

"In the spring, I mean, when the hunt is over."

"Not come back," Attean repeated. "Not live in village again. Our people find new hunting ground."

"But this is your home!"

"My people hunters. My grandfather say many white men come soon. Cut down trees. Make house. Plant corn. Where my people hunt?"

What could Matt answer to this? He had only one argument to offer. "Your grandfather wants you to learn to read," he reminded Attean. "I haven't been much of a teacher. But when my family comes it will be different. My mother will teach you to read, and to write too."

"What for I read? My grandfather mighty hunter. My father mighty hunter. They not read."

"Your grandfather wants you to be able to understand treaties," Matt insisted.

"We go far away. No more white man. Not need to sign paper."

An uncomfortable doubt had long been troubling

Matt. Now, before Attean went away, he had to know. "This land," he said slowly, "this place where my father built his cabin. Did it belong to your grandfather? Did he own it once?"

"How one man own ground?" Attean questioned.

"Well, my father owns it now. He bought it."

"I not understand." Attean scowled. "How can man own land? Land same as air. Land for all people to live on. For beaver and deer. Does deer own land?"

How could you explain, Matt wondered, to someone who did not want to understand? Somewhere in the back of his mind there was a sudden suspicion that Attean was making sense and he was not. It was better not to talk about it. Instead he asked, "Where will you go?"

"My grandfather say much forest where sun go down. White man not come so far."

To the west. Matt had heard his father talk about the west. There was good land there for the taking. Some of their neighbors in Quincy had chosen to go west instead of buying land in Maine. How could he tell Attean that there would be white men there too? Still, they said there was no end of land in the west. He reckoned there must be enough for both white men and Indians. Before he could think what to say, Attean spoke again.

"I give you gift," he said. "Dog like you. I tell him stay with you."

"You mean you're not taking him with you?"

"No good for hunt," Attean said. "Walk slow now. Good for stay here with *medabe* — with white brother."

Attean's careless words did not deceive Matt. He knew very well how Attean felt about that no-good dog that followed him everywhere he went.

And Attean had said white brother!

Matt could not find the words he needed, but he knew there was something he must do. He had to have a gift for Attean. And he had nothing to give, nothing at all that belonged to him. *Robinson Crusoe*? What could that mean to a boy who would never now learn to read it?

He did have one thing. At the thought of it, something twisted tight in his stomach. But it was the only thing he had that could possibly match the gifts Attean had given him.

"Wait here," he told Attean. He went into the cabin and took down the tin box. The watch was ticking away inside it. He had never forgotten to wind it, even when he was too tired to notch a stick. Now he lifted it out and held it in his hand, the way he had held it when his father had given it to him, as though it were a fragile bird's egg. His father would never understand. Before he could think about it another minute, Matt hurried back to where Attean stood waiting.

"I have a gift for you," he said. "It tells the time of day. I'll show you how to wind it up."

Attean held the watch even more carefully. There was no mistaking that he was pleased and impressed. Probably, Matt thought, Attean would never learn to use it. The sun and the shadows of the trees told him all he needed to know about the time of day. But Attean knew that Matt's gift was important.

"Fine gift," he said. He put the watch very gently

into his pouch. Then he held out his hand. Awkwardly, the two boys shook hands.

"Your father come soon," Attean said.

"I hope you get the biggest moose in Maine," Matt answered.

Attean turned and walked into the woods. The dog sprang up to follow him. Attean motioned him back and uttered one stern order. Puzzled, the dog sank down and put his chin between his paws. As Attean walked away, he whined softly, but he obeyed. Matt knelt down and put his hand on the dog's head.

❦CHAPTER 23❧

MATT FILLED HIS DAYS WITH WORK. HE MADE THE cabin trim. Where the clay had dried and crumbled away between the logs, he brought new mud, strengthened it with pebbles, and packed the spaces tightly. On the inside he chinked every tiny crack to make the room snug. The pile of logs stacked against the cabin wall grew steadily higher.

His meager harvest was safely stored away. The corn, the little he had managed to save from the deer and crows, had all been shucked. Sitting by the fire after his supper, he scraped the dried kernels from the cobs, remembering the many long evenings at home when he and his sister Sarah had been set to the same work with a corn scraper. Sarah would laugh now to see him rubbing away with an old clamshell like an Indian. Some of the ears of corn he had hung against the wall, by the twisted husks, as he had seen his mother do. She had said once they were like scraps of sunshine in the dark days. Overhead he hung strips of pumpkin on ropes of vine strung from wall to wall. They would be ready for his mother to make into pies.

In a corner leaned the old flour sack, overflowing with the nuts he had gathered, hickory and butternut, and even the acorns he had once thought proper food only for squirrels. On the shelf ranged birch baskets filled with dried berries and the wild cranberries he had discovered shining like jewels along the boggy shores of the pond. They were puckery to the tongue, but when his mother came she would bring sugar, and the stewed cranberries would make a fine treat with her bread of white flour.

Matt forced himself to eat sparingly of these things. The corn he regarded as a sort of trust. His father had planted it, and would be counting on it to feed the family through the winter. And some must be saved for the spring planting. Proud though he was of his harvest, Matt knew in his heart that it was far from enough. The hunt for food would be never-ending.

Hour after hour, with his bow, Matt tramped through the forest, the dog beside him. There was not much game to hunt these days. More often than not, his snares were empty. Soon the animals would be buried deep in burrows. Twice he had glimpsed a caribou moving through the trees, but he had little hope of bringing down any large animal with his light arrows. Once in a long while he succeeded in shooting a duck or a muskrat. The squirrels were too quick for him. Although the dog was certainly not much of a hunter, he did occasionally track down some small creature. But he also had to eat his share, sometimes more than his share, because Matt could not resist those beseeching eyes. Truth to tell, they were both hungry much of the time.

Luckily, they would not starve with the pond and creeks teeming with fish. Matt knew that for many months of the year fish filled the Indian cookpots. Luckily too, fish were easy to catch, though Matt had to be continually twisting and splicing new lines from vines and spruce roots. Mornings, now, he had to shatter a skim of ice on the pond. Soon he would have to cut holes with his axe and let his lines down deep. He shivered to think of it.

It was the cold that bothered him most. His home-spun jacket was still sound, since he had had little use for it in the warm weather. But his breeches were threadbare. One knee showed naked through a gaping hole, and the frayed legs stopped a good five inches above his ankles. His linen shirt was thin as a page of his father's Bible, and so small for him that it threatened to split every time he moved. Even inside the cabin he was scarcely warm enough. The moment he ventured outside his teeth chattered. He thought enviously of the Indians' deerskin leggings. But a deer was far beyond his prowess as a hunter.

There were two blankets on his pine bed, his father's and his own. Why couldn't one of them cover him in the daytime as well as in the night? He spread a blanket out on the floor and hacked it with his axe and his knife, using his worn-out breeches as a pattern. From the leftover scraps he carefully pulled threads and twisted them together. He had seen the Indian women using bone needles, and he searched about outside the cabin till he found some thin, hard bits of bone. These he shaved down with his knife. He ruined three bits trying to poke a hole through the bone, before he thought to try a thin slit instead to hold the thread. Finally he managed to sew his woolen pieces together. He thrust his legs into the shapeless breeches and gathered the top about his waist with a bit of rope. He was mighty pleased with himself. He was going to be forever hauling them up, and they were sure to trip him if he had to run, but at least he could kneel on the ice and pull in his lines.

From two rabbit skins he made some mittens without thumbs. He had no stockings, and his moosehide moccasins were wearing thin. He decided he could stuff them with scraps of blanket or even with duck feathers. He remembered that once, in a downpour, Attean had shown him how to line his moccasins with dried moss to soak up the rain. Perhaps moss could soak up the cold as well, and there was plenty of it about.

His most satisfying achievement was his fur hat. For this he knew he must have more fur. In the woods Attean had once pointed out to him a deadfall, constructed of heavy logs so intricately balanced that they would fall with deadly accuracy on an animal that attempted to steal the bait inside. Beaver and otter were caught in such traps, Attean explained, sometimes even bear. Now Matt determined to make one for himself. Perhaps a small one. It would take a very large log even to stun a strong animal, and he had no wish to come upon a wounded bear. Much as he would like a bearskin, he would try for a smaller animal.

He felled and trimmed two good-sized trees. Setting the logs on lighter posts was a feat of delicate balance that took him hours of patient trial and error. Over and over they crashed down, threatening his toes and fingers. Finally they held to his satisfaction, and gingerly he slipped three fish inside the trap.

To his astonishment, on the third morning he found an animal lying under the fallen logs, so nearly dead that it was no task to club it. It was smaller than the otters he had seen playing along the banks. A fisher, perhaps?

That night he and the dog feasted on crackling bits of roast meat. It was strong-flavored, and he knew the Indians did not care to eat it, but he could not be so choosy. Other strips he hung over the fire to smoke. There was also a scant amount of yellow fat. Used sparingly, a spoonful of that fat would make his usual fish diet taste like a banquet. The real treasure was the pelt, heavy and lustrous. He worked on it slowly, as he had watched the Indian women work. With a sharp-edged stone he scraped away every trace of fat and flesh from the skin, washed it in the creek, and for days, in his spare hours, rubbed and stretched it to make it soft and pliable. Then he set to work with his bone needle. He was enormously proud of the cap he fashioned. Saknis himself would have envied it.

Most of this work he had done by firelight. He longed for candles. He ate his supper by the light of split pine branches set in a crack in the chimney. They gave light aplenty, but they smoked and dripped sticky pitch, and he was always afraid he might drop off to sleep and wake up to find the log chimney afire. At any rate, after a day of chopping and tramping he was tired enough to go to bed with the dark.

So often, as he did the squaw work that Attean would

have despised, thoughts of his mother filled his head. He imagined her moving about the cabin, humming her little tunes as she beat up a batch of corn bread, shaking out the boardcloth at the door – for of course she would not let them eat at a bare table. He could see her sitting by the firelight in the evening, her knitting needles clicking as she made a woolen sock for him. Sometimes he could almost hear the sound of her voice, and when he shut his eyes he could see her special smile.

He tried to think of ways to please her. She would need new dishes for the good meals she would cook. He whittled out four wooden trenchers and four clean new bowls, rubbing them smooth with sand from the creek. He made a little brush to clean them with from a birch sapling, carefully splitting the ends into thin fibers. In the same way, he made a sturdy birch broom to sweep the floor. Then he set himself a more difficult task, a cradle for the baby. With only an axe and his knife, the work took all his patience. His first attempts were fit only for kindling. But when the cradle was done he was proud of it. It was clumsy, perhaps, but it rocked without bumping, and there wasn't a splinter anywhere to harm a baby's skin. Sitting by the fire, it seemed a promise that soon his family would be there. When he had a few more rabbit skins he would make a soft coverlet.

For Sarah he made a cornhusk doll with cornsilk hair. He was surprised at how much he looked forward to Sarah's coming. Back at home she had been nothing but a pesky child, always following him about and pestering him to be taken along wherever he was going.

Now he remembered the way she had run to meet him when he came home from school, pigtails flying, eyes shining, demanding to know everything that had happened there. Sarah hated fiercely being a girl and having no school to go to. She would be full of curiosity in the forest. She wasn't afraid like most girls. She was spunky enough to try almost anything. She was like that Indian girl, Attean's sister. What a pity they couldn't have known each other!

~CHAPTER 24~

MATT STOOD LOOKING UP AT THE SKY OVER THE clearing. "It's going to snow," he told the dog. "You can feel it, can't you?" The dog lifted its nose, testing the promise in the air.

Matt reckoned he had been lucky so far. The heavy snows had not come. There had been flurries, thin and swirling, sifting through the trees. Many mornings he had waked to find a coating of white on the cabin roof, which would melt away under the noonday sun. Today everything seemed different. The sky was the color of his mother's pewter plate. The brown withered leaves of the oak trees hung motionless from the branches. Three crows searched noisily among the dry cornstalks. A flock of small birds hopped nervously under the pines.

"It's almost Christmas," he said out loud. He could not remember for sure how many weeks belonged to each month. Sometimes he was not even certain that he had remembered to cut a notch every day. Each day was so like the day before, and Christmas Day, when it came, would not have anything to mark it from all the others. He tried to put out of his mind the thought of his mother's Christmas pudding.

"We'd better get in extra firewood," he said, and the dog scrambled eagerly after him.

Late in the day the snow began, soundlessly, steadily. Before dark it had laid a white blanket over the trees and the stumps and the cabin. When Matt and the dog went outside at bedtime the chilly whiteness reached over his moccasins and closed around his bare ankles. They were both thankful to hurry inside again.

Next morning, in the darkness of the cabin, Matt made his way to the door. He could scarcely push it open. The bank of snow outside reached almost to the latch. He stared at it in alarm. Was he going to be a prisoner in his own cabin? With all his preparations, he had never thought of a shovel. His axe would be about as much use as a teaspoon. He set himself to hewing a slab of firewood to make some sort of blade. By the time he had dug a few feet of pathway, the sun was high. He stepped into a dazzling white world.

Now at last he could make use of the snowshoes that hung on the cabin wall. Eagerly he strapped the bindings about his legs and climbed up out of the narrow path he had dug. The snowshoes held him lightly; he stood poised on the snow like a duck on water. But with his first steps he discovered that he could not even waddle like a duck on land. The clumsy hoops got in each other's way, one of them forever getting trapped beneath the other. All at once he got the knack of it, and he wanted to shout out loud.

He tramped from one of his snares to another, waiting every few moments for the dog who floundered happily behind him. The snares were buried deep, and empty, and he set them higher, just in case some animal might venture out of its burrow. Then he tramped all the way to the pond for the sheer pleasure of it. Coming back through the woods he marveled at his own tracks, like the claw prints of a giant bird. Suddenly he realized that he was happy, as he had never been in the weeks since Attean had gone away. He was no longer afraid of the winter ahead. The snowshoes had set him free.

The cabin was warm and welcoming. He melted snow in his kettle and made a tea of tips of hemlock. He shelled and crushed a handful of acorns and boiled them with a strip of pumpkin. Afterwards, for the first time in weeks, he took down *Robinson Crusoe*. Reading by the firelight, he felt drowsy and contented. Life on a warm island in the Pacific might be easier, but tonight Matt thought that he wouldn't for a moment have given up his snug cabin buried in the snow.

CHAPTER 25

THREE DAYS LATER SNOW THREATENED AGAIN, AND
Matt gathered a pile of firewood to dry inside. He had
just carried in his third armful when he heard the dog
barking frantically a short distance away. Matt found
him standing on the bank of the creek, his feet braced,
the ridge of hair standing up along his back. Peering
along the creek, Matt caught his breath. Something
dark was moving along the frozen course of the stream,
a huge shape, too large to be an animal, even a moose.
Then he saw it was a man, dragging behind him some
sort of sled. He didn't move like an Indian. As he
watched, Matt made out a second, smaller shape just
coming into sight around the bend of the creek.

He did not dare to shout for fear they would vanish
like ghosts. He stood still, his heart pounding. Then
finally he began to run.

"Pa!" he choked. "Pa!"

His father flung down the pack he carried. His arms
went round Matt and held fast, though he could not
manage to speak a word. Then Matt saw his mother,
struggling to climb down from the sled. He bent and
threw his arms around her. How small she seemed,
even under the heavy cloak. Sarah came floundering

through the snow in her father's footsteps and stood staring at him, her eyes bright under the woolen hood. She wasn't the child he remembered. Awkwardly he put his arms around her and gave her a hug.

Then they were all talking at once, trying to be heard over the fierce clamor of the dog.

"Quiet!" Matt shouted at him. "This is my family! They've come! They're actually here!"

They pushed their way through the snow to the cabin, leaving the sled where it stood in the middle of the ice. Matt helped his mother over the doorstep. He could see she was scarcely able to stand, and he pulled a stool nearer the fire for her. She clung to him, her eyes on his face. Matt would hardly have recognized her, so thin and pale, with great shadows under her eyes. But those eyes were warm and shining, and her smile was as beautiful as he had remembered.

"I was bound we'd get here 'fore Christmas," she panted. "I couldn't of borne it to let Christmas go by. Oh Matt — you're safe!"

"It was the typhus," his father explained. "We all took sick with it, and the fever was bad. Takes all the strength out of a body. Your ma got took the worst. We'd ought to of waited longer till she was more fit, but she was dead set on starting. The river is 'most frozen shut. We had to wait at the trading post three weeks before anyone would risk carrying us. Then we had to get the sled made. But your ma, she kept pushing at us. She's a rare one, your ma."

"I had to," she said. "Thinking of you alone in this place."

"It wasn't so bad," Matt said stoutly. "I wasn't alone all the time. I had the Indians."

"Indians!" his mother gasped. "Are there Indians hereabouts?"

"Pa said there wouldn't be," Sarah exclaimed, wide-eyed. "What are they like?"

"They're gone now," Matt said. "But they were my friends." Then he brought it out proudly. "I had an Indian brother."

From the way they stared at him, he could see it was going to take a mighty lot of explaining before they could understand. He didn't suppose they ever would, truly. His father said nothing. He was looking soberly at the snowshoes propped against the wall and at the bow hanging over the door where the rifle should have been. Everywhere he looked, Matt realized, he must see something the Indians had given him or had taught him how to make for himself. However, his father seemed to think there was no time now for questions.

"We'd better unpack the sled," he said, "before it starts to snow again."

Matt sprang to help. There was one question he had not dared to ask till he and his father were alone. "The baby — did you leave it behind?"

His father ran a hand over his beard. His eyes were troubled. "The little one only lived five days," he answered. "'Twas a pitiful little thing would never have made this journey. Just don't say aught to your ma. She still takes it hard."

Matt promised. He wished he had somehow been able to hide the cradle before she noticed it.

Standing in the snow, his father reached to put a hand on Matt's shoulder. "You've done a grown man's job, son," he said. "I'm right proud of you."

Matt could not speak. It took his breath away to think that he might have gone with the Indians, that they might have come to an empty cabin and found that all his mother's fears had come true. He would never have heard the words his father had just spoken. This was how Attean had felt, he knew, when he had found his manitou and become a hunter.

As his father untied the bundles from the sledge, Matt lugged them into the cabin. Flour. Molasses. A fine new kettle. Warm, bright quilts. And, thanks be, new boots for him and a woolen jacket and breeches. He felt richer than Robinson Crusoe with all the plunder from that sunken ship. Then he noted that his father had a new rifle, and presently he discovered, poking out from his mother's pack, his own old musket. He hadn't a doubt she had learned to use it, and would have too, had her family been threatened. He suspected that even Sarah, so grown-up now, wouldn't have feared to pull that trigger if there'd been need of it. Well, there'd be no more need of it now, with two men to fend for them.

Inside the cabin Sarah was bustling capably about, unwrapping the pewter dishes, setting out the little whale-oil lamp that had always stood on the table in Quincy.

"That's the funniest-looking dog I ever saw," she said. "It won't come near us."

"He's an Indian dog," Matt told her. "He's suspicious of white folks. You wait. You'll get to like him."

He couldn't get over how much older she looked. But still spunky. Her eyes were sparkling, and Matt suspected that for her the long journey had just been an adventure. He should have made her a bow instead of a doll, and he would, too, the first chance he got.

His mother had thrown off her cloak, and the fire had brought a bit of color into her cheeks. She was making a great show of coming home. If the cabin seemed rough and cramped after the pretty house she had left behind, she never let on for a moment. She went about admiring everything — the drying ears of corn, the strings of pumpkin, the fine new wooden bowls he had carved.

"All this food," she marveled. "And I've been feared you were starving!"

He was thankful now for the times he had gone hungry to save what he could for their coming. "There's jerky for supper," he told her. "I tried not to eat too much of it. You can make a pretty fair stew with that and a little pumpkin. Some salt would sure help if you brought any."

As he started out again, his mother stopped him and put her hands on his shoulders. "Wait a minute," she said. "I just want to look at you." She had to tip her head back to do it. "You look different, Matt. You're 'most as tall as your pa. And awful thin. You're so brown I'd have taken you for an Indian."

"I almost was one," he said, giving her a quick hug to show he was joking. He hoped she'd never know how true it was.

"We're going to have neighbors," she said happily, as

she set the new kettle over the fire. "A man and his wife have a claim not five miles from here. They're staying at the trading post till spring. We plan to share a pair of oxen. They say three other families are coming too. They're going to set up a mill. 'Fore you know it we'll have a town here, maybe even a school for you children."

Neighbors. That was a thought that would take some getting used to. Matt supposed he ought to be pleased. Yes, of course he was pleased. It was just that he rather liked it as it was here in the forest. With all the gladness in him right now, you wouldn't think there'd be room for any other thought. But even now, with his family here, their voices filling the long silence, with all his worries vanishing like smoke up the chimney, he suddenly thought of the Indians. He wished that Attean and his grandfather could know that he had been right to stay, that his father had come as he had promised them. But the old man had been right, too. More white men were coming. There would be a town here on the land where the Indians had hunted the caribou and the beaver. If only he could be sure that the Indians had found a new hunting ground.

Matt thrust his arms into his new jacket and went out again into the snow. Behind him the cabin glowed, warm and filled with life. Already steam was rising from the new kettle. He'd cook one of his special stews for them for supper, and he wouldn't have to eat it alone. They would all sit together around the table and bow their heads while his father asked the blessing.

Then he would tell them about Attean.

THE SIGN OF THE BEAVER
by Elizabeth George Speare

Beware: Indians! Wild animals! Strangers!

Until the day his father returns to their cabin in the Maine wilderness, twelve-year-old Matt must try to survive on his own. Although Matt is brave, he's not prepared for an attack by swarming bees, and he's astonished when he's rescued by an Indian chief and his grandson, Attean.

As the boys come to know each other Attean learns to speak English while Matt becomes a skilled hunter. Though many months have passed, there's no sign of Matt's family. Then Attean asks Matt to join the Beaver tribe and move north. Should Matt abandon his hopes of ever seeing his family again and move on to a new life?

Best Books of the Year   *—The New York Times*

An ALA Notable Book

"A sturdy, never faltering story of wilderness survival…"   *—Kirkus Reviews*

"The story has flow and pace, good style, and that careful but unobtrusive research that marks the best historical fiction."   *—Bulletin of the Center for Children's Books*

"Distinguished in style and compelling in narrative force… As usual in Mrs. Speare's novels, each word rings true."   *—The New York Times Book Review*

ELIZABETH GEORGE SPEARE has also written *The Witch of Blackbird Pond*, available in a Dell Yearling edition. She lives in Easton, Connecticut.

A Yearling Book
Dell Publishing
New York

RL: 5.7
010–014
0-440-80038-2